I0613022

Horatio Alger

A Boy's Fortune

The Strange Adventures of Ben Baker

Horatio Alger

A Boy's Fortune
The Strange Adventures of Ben Baker

ISBN/EAN: 9783337341275

Printed in Europe, USA, Canada, Australia, Japan

Cover: Foto ©Andreas Hilbeck / pixelio.de

More available books at **www.hansebooks.com**

A BOY'S FORTUNE

OR, THE

STRANGE ADVENTURES OF BEN BAKER

BY

HORATIO ALGER, JR.

AUTHOR OF "ADRIFT IN THE CITY," "GRIT," "FRANK AND FEARLESS,"
"DAN, THE DETECTIVE," "PLUCKY PAUL PALMER," ETC.

THE JOHN C. WINSTON CO.
PHILADELPHIA
CHICAGO   TORONTO

COPYRIGHT, 1898, BY

HENRY T. COATES & CO.

CONTENTS.

iv CONTENTS.

A BOY'S FORTUNE;

OR, THE

STRANGE ADVENTURES OF BEN BAKER.

CHAPTER I.

OLIVER HITCHCOCK'S LUNCH-ROOM.

"WAKE up there! This is no place to sleep."

The speaker was a policeman, the scene was City Hall Park, and the person addressed was a boy of perhaps sixteen, who was reclining on one of the park benches, with a bundle at his side.

The officer accompanied his admonition with a shaking which served to arouse the young sleeper.

"Is it morning?" asked the boy, drowsily, not yet realizing his situation.

"No, it isn't. Don't you know where you are?"

"I know now," said the boy, looking about him.

"Come, get up, Johnny! This is no place for you," said the officer, not unkindly, for he was a family man, and had a boy of his own not far from the age of the young wayfarer.

The boy got up, and looked about him undecidedly. Clearly he did not know where to go.

"Are you a stranger in the city?" asked the policeman.

"Yes, sir. I only got here this afternoon."

"Then you have no place to sleep?"

"No."

"Haven't you got money enough to go to a hotel? There is Leggett's Hotel, just down Park Row," pointing eastward.

"I have a little money, but I can't afford to go to a hotel."

"You can go to the Newsboys' Lodging House for six cents."

"Where is it?"

The officer told him.

"I feel hungry. I suppose there isn't any place where I can get supper so late as this?"

"Oh, yes! There's one close by. Do you see a light over there?"

The officer pointed to a basement opposite the post-office, at the corner of Beekman street and Park Row.

"Yes, I see it," answered the boy. "Is it a good place?"

"I should say so. Why, that's Oll Hitchcock's. You can't get a better cup of coffee or sandwich anywhere in New York. I often get lunch there myself, when I don't have time to go home."

"Thank you for telling me. I'll go over."

Ben Baker, for that is the name of our young hero, walked across the street, and descended the steps into the well-known restaurant or lunch-room of Oliver Hitchcock. Open by night as well as by day, there is hardly an hour of the twenty-four in which it is not fairly well patronized, while at times it is thronged. It is a favorite resort for men of all classes— printers, journalists, newsmen—who drop in in the early morning on their way to or from the offices of the great morning papers for their regular supplies—politicians and business men of all kinds.

More than once in Oliver Hitchcock's old saloon, farther up the same street, Horace Greeley, the elder Bennett, and Raymond, of the *Times*, could be found at the plain tables, unprovided with cloths, but bearing appetizing dishes.

When Ben entered the restaurant at half-past eleven he was surprised to find most of the tables occupied.

Coming from the country, where ten o'clock found nearly every one in bed, he was much surprised to find so many persons up and engaged in supping.

"People in New York seem to sit up all night," he thought.

He took a vacant seat, and the waiter soon coming up to him, stood in silent expectation of an order.

"Give me a cup of coffee and a sandwich," said Ben.

"What kind?"

"Ham."

The waiter sped on his errand, and soon set

before our hero a cup of fragrant coffee, steam-
ing hot, and a sandwich made of tender meat
and fresh bread, which tasted delicious to the
hungry boy—so delicious that he resolved to
forego the intended piece of pie and ordered
another.

While he was eating the second sandwich,
he observed that a young man, sitting just opposite, was eyeing him attentively.

He was tall, dark-complexioned, slender,
and had a kindly face.

"You seem to relish your supper, Johnny,"
he said.

"Yes, I do, but my name isn't Johnny."

The young man smiled.

"Excuse me," he said, "but in New York
we call boys by that name, if we don't know
their real names. I suppose you have not been
here long?"

"No; I only arrived this afternoon."

"Come to make your fortune, eh?"

"Well, I don't know. I should like to, but
if I can make a living it is all I expect. Besides, I have another object," added the boy,
slowly.

" Were you ever here before ?"

" No, sir."

" You are up rather late. You don't sit up so late in the country, do you ?"

" Oh, no, I am in bed by nine o'clock generally."

" We don't go to bed early here. I myself haven't been in bed before midnight for three years."

" Do you like to sit up so late ?" asked Ben.

" I didn't at first. Now I am used to it. My business keeps me up late."

Seeing that Ben looked curious, he added:

" I am a reporter on a morning paper."

" Do you like it ?" asked Ben, doubtfully.

" Oh, yes. It isn't a bad business."

" What paper do you write for ?" asked Ben, with considerable respect for a man who wrote for the papers.

" I used to work on the *Sun*. Now I'm on the *Herald*. It suits me very well while I am a young man, but I should like a different position when I am older."

" Is it hard work ?"

" Sometimes. I am liable to be sent off at

five minutes' notice to any part of the city.
Then I am expected to keep my eyes open,
and make note of anything that comes in my
way. There was a big fire last night about
one o'clock, up town. I heard of it as I was
going up in the horse-cars, so I hurried to the
spot, and instead of going to bed I got all the
information I could, hurried back to the office
and wrote it up. I got extra pay for it. Besides, it shows interest, and may help me to
promotion."

"Have you got through for to-night?" asked
Ben.

"Yes; I feel tired, being up so late last
night. When I leave here I shall go home
and to bed. By the way, where are you staying?"

"Nowhere," answered Ben, in some embar-
rassment.

"You are not going to sit up all night, are
you?"

"No. I suppose I must go somewhere."

"There is a hotel close by—Leggett's."

"So a policeman told me, but I haven't
much money, and I had better not go to a

hotel. He said there was a Newsboys' Lodging House, where I could get lodging for six cents."

"I am afraid you couldn't get in at this late hour."

Ben looked perplexed. He felt sleepy, and needed rest.

"Then I suppose I shall have to go to the hotel," he answered. "Do you know how much they charge ?"

"Not exactly. It depends on the room. I can direct you to a cheaper lodging even than you could get at the Newsboys' Lodging House."

"I wish you would," said Ben, looking up hopefully.

"Then come home with me. My room-mate is away for a few days, and I have room for you."

"Thank you, sir, if it won't inconvenience you."

"Not at all."

Ben had read of adventurers that lie in wait for unsuspecting travellers and "rope them in," but he entertained no suspicion of the young man who had so kindly offered him a bed. The mere fact that he was a newspaper man seemed to Ben a guarantee of respectability.

As Hugh Manton (the reporter) and he went up to the counter to pay the amount of their checks, a stout, handsomely-dressed man, of portly form and medium stature, entered the restaurant. As his eye fell upon Ben he started and muttered to himself:

"That boy in New York! What does he want here?"

CHAPTER II.

A LODGING IN ST. MARK'S PLACE.

HUGH MANTON, whose calling had trained him to quick observation, did not fail to notice that the stout gentleman was in some way moved by the sight of his young companion. This surprised him not a little, for in the portly gentleman he recognized a wealthy retail merchant whose store was located on the upper part of Broadway.

"Can there be any connection between this country boy and the rich Mr. Walton?" he asked himself, curiously.

He resolved to take an early opportunity to question Ben.

When their bills were paid they went out of the restaurant. It was twelve o'clock by the clock on the City Hall when they emerged from the lunch-room. A Third Avenue horse car was just passing.

"Follow me!" said the reporter, as he jumped aboard.

Ben did so.

"My room is on St. Mark's place," he said. "I suppose you don't know where that is?"

"No; I have never been in New York before."

"It must be nearly two miles from the City Hall Park. It is the eastern part of Eighth street."

"Fare!" said the conductor.

Ben put his hand into his pocket.

"No," said his companion, "I have the change."

"Thank you!" said Ben, "but you ought not to pay for me."

"Oh, you shall take your turn some time."

They sat down in the car, and, both being tired, sat silent.

After riding fifteen to twenty minutes they came in sight of a large brown-colored building, set between Third and Fourth avenues, just beyond the termination of the Bowery.

"We will get out here," said Hugh Manton. "That building is the Cooper Institute. Of course you have heard of it? We turn to the right, and will soon reach my den."

Time was when St. Mark's place had some
pretension to gentility, but now it is given up
to lodging and boarding-houses. In front of
a brick house, between Second and First avenues, the reporter paused.

"This is where I live," he said.

He opened the door with a latch-key, and
they entered a dark hall, for at eleven o'clock
the light was extinguished.

"Follow me," he said to Ben. "Take
hold of the banister, and feel your way. I
am generally the last in," he said, "unless
some one of my fellow-lodgers is out having a
good time. One more flight of stairs. So,
here we are."

The rear room on the third floor was his.
Opening a door, he quickly lighted a gas-jet
on one side of the room.

"There, my young friend," said the reporter, "you can undress as soon as you
please, and jump into that bed nearest the
window. It isn't luxurious, but will serve
your turn."

"Thank you," said Ben. "I feel very
tired. I shan't lie awake long to consider

what kind of a bed I am in. Do you get up early?"

"Sometimes I get up as early as nine o'clock."

Ben laughed.

"Do you call that early?" he said. "Six o'clock isn't extra early in the country."

"My young friend—by the way, what's your name?"

"Ben Baker."

"Well, Ben, let me tell you that nine o'clock is a very early hour for a reporter. We'll rise at nine, and go out to breakfast together."

"I think I can sleep till then," said Ben, "for I am as tired as I ever was after a hard day's work on the farm."

* * * * * * *

"Wake up, Ben."

It was the next morning and the words were spoken by Hugh Manton, as he gave a gentle shake to the still sleeping boy.

Ben opened his eyes and looked about him in a confused way. Finally recollection came to him.

"I thought I was in that park down town," he said, with a smile.

"Do you know where you are now?"

"Yes."

"Have you slept well, youngster?"

"I have had a bully sleep."

"And you feel ready for breakfast?"

"I think I can eat some."

The two new acquaintances dressed and went down stairs. Ben was about to take his bundle, but the reporter stopped him.

"Leave it here," he said, "for the present. Blodgett won't be back for three or four days, and you can stay here till he returns. You won't want to be lugging that bundle all over town."

"You are very kind," said Ben, gratefully.

"Why shouldn't I be? I came to the city myself a poor country youth, and I had a hard struggle as first till I reached my present pinnacle of wealth," he concluded, with a smile.

"Are reporters well paid?" asked Ben, innocently.

"That depends! Whatever they earn, it is seldom that one gets fifty dollars ahead.

That is because, as a rule, they are improvident, and sometimes dissipated. I am not as well paid as some, but I make a little writing sketches for the weekly story papers. I pick up two or three hundred a year that way. Then I take better care of my money than some. I laid up five hundred dollars last year, and nearly as much the year before."

"You will soon be rich," said Ben, to whom five hundred dollars seemed a large sum of money.

The reporter smiled.

"It takes considerable money to make a man rich in New York," he said. "However, I know it makes me feel very comfortable to think I have a thousand dollars in the bank."

"I should think it would," said Ben, seriously.

"Here we are!" said the reporter, pausing in front of a restaurant on Ninth street, facing the side of the great retail store established by the late A. T. Stewart. "We can get a comfortable breakfast inside for a low price."

They entered, and sat down at one of the small tables. Hugh Manton ordered a beefsteak and a cup of coffee. This, with bread and butter, cost twenty cents. Ben duplicated the order. The meat was not of the best quality, but it was as good as could be afforded at the price, and Ben ate with the zest of a healthy boy of his age.

"By the way, Ben," said the reporter, with apparent carelessness, though he scanned the face of his young companion attentively as he spoke, "are you acquainted with a clothing merchant of this city named Nicholas Walton?"

Ben started in irrepressible astonishment.

"What makes you ask?" he said. "Did you know he was my uncle?"

It was Hugh Manton's turn to be astonished.

"Your uncle!" he exclaimed. "You don't mean to say Nicholas Walton is your uncle?"

"Yes, I do. My mother is his sister."

"Is it possible? He has the reputation of being very rich, while you——"

"While I am very poor. Yes, that is true."

"Are you going to call upon him?"

"Yes. I thought, being my uncle, he might give me a place in his store."

" Did you write him that you were coming?"

" No—that is, not lately. I wrote three months ago, and he wrote back that I had better stay where I was."

"What were you doing?"

" I was working on a farm. I was paid three dollars a week."

" Did you live on the farm?"

" No; I lived with my mother."

" She is living, then?"

" Yes," said Ben, and his face lighted up with love for his absent mother.

" I should think Mr. Walton would do something for his own sister."

"So he does. He sends her twenty-five dollars a month. She lives in a small house belonging to my grandfather. My uncle is part owner, but he lets mother live in it."

" I suppose you don't like the country, or you wouldn't have come to the city."

" I have a taste for business, and no taste for farming. My uncle came to New York a poor boy, and he has succeeded. I don't see why I can't."

" It doesn't always follow," said the reporter,

thoughtfully. "Still I think you have it in you to succeed. You look bold, persevering and resolute."

"I mean to succeed!" said Ben, firmly. "I am not afraid of work."

"Shall you call on your uncle this morning?"

"Yes; I want to find out as soon as I can what I am to depend upon."

"Very well! Just make my room your home. I shall not be back myself till midnight, or later, but here is a latch-key which will admit you to my room whenever you like. I have Blodgett's with me, which I can use myself."

CHAPTER III.

THE MERCHANT'S SECRET.

FIVE years before Ben's arrival in the city Nicholas Walton kept a moderate sized store on Grand street. He was doing a good business, but he was not satisfied. He wished to take a store on Broadway, and make his name prominent among business men. In this wish his wife entirely sympathized with him. She boasted aristocratic lineage, but when Mr. Walton married her she was living in genteel poverty, while her mother was forced, very much against her will, to take lodgers. It was a great piece of good luck for Theodosia Granville to marry a prosperous young merchant like Nicholas Walton, but she chose to consider that all the indebtedness was on the other side, and was fond of talking about the sacrifice she made in marrying a man of no family.

They had two children, Emiline and Clar-

ence Plantagenet Walton, the latter about
three months older than his cousin Ben. Both
were haughty and arrogant in temper and disposition, and as a matter of course neither was
a favorite with their young associates, though
each had flatterers whose interest was served
by subserviency.

At that time Ben's father was living and
practicing as a physician in the little town of
Sunderland, fifty miles distant in the country.
There was comparatively little intercourse between the families, though there was not yet
that difference in their worldly circumstances
that afterward arose.

One day, just as the clerks were getting
ready to close up, Nicholas Walton was surprised by the sudden appearance of his brother-
in-law, Dr. Baker.

"What brings you to town, James?" he
asked.

"Business of great importance," answered
Baker.

"Indeed!" said Walton, curiously.

"I will tell you all about it, but not here."

"Do you go back to Sunderland to-night?"

"No; I think of trespassing upon your hospitality."

"Certainly. I shall be glad to have you stay with me. My wife and children are out of town—visiting a sister of hers in Hartford—but the servants will see that we are comfortable."

"All the better. Of course I should have been glad to see Mrs. Walton and the children, but now you can give me more attention."

"I wonder whether he wants to borrow money," thought the merchant, with some uneasiness. "If he does, I shall refuse as civilly as I can. I don't propose to be a prey to impecunious relatives. I need all the money I can command to further my own schemes. In three or four years, if things go well, I shall be able to move to Broadway, and then our family can take a higher social position. My wife would like to have me move at once, but I don't choose to do anything rashly. The time has not yet come for so important a step."

"We will go now," said Mr. Walton. "The clerks will close up. If you will walk as far as the Bowery, we will board a Fourth avenue car."

"Do you still live on Twelfth street, Nicholas?"

"Yes. Mrs. Walton urges me to take a house on Madison avenue, but I must not go too fast."

"You are prospering, I take it, Nicholas?"

"He is feeling his way toward a loan, I am afraid," thought the merchant.

"Yes, I am making headway," he admitted, warily, "but I have to be very cautious. Oftentimes I am short of money, I assure you. In fact, I am hampered by my small capital."

"My neighbors in Sunderland would be surprised to hear that," said Dr. Baker, smiling. "They look upon you as one of the merchant princes of New York."

"Do they?" said Walton, looking gratified. "Some day I hope to be what they think I am now."

"You will be, if you are not too much in haste."

"So I hope. And you, I hope you are prospering?" said the merchant, guardedly.

"I have no cause for complaint," said his brother-in-law, "especially now."

"What does he mean by 'especially now?'" thought the merchant.

"I am glad to hear it," he said, aloud.

Arrived at the house in Twelfth street—it was a plain brick house of three stories—dinner was found to be awaiting, and as they sat down at once, there was no opportunity for a private conversation. When the cloth was removed, and they were left to themselves, Walton invited his brother-in-law's confidence by saying, suggestively :

"So business of importance brought you to New York, doctor?"

"Yes, business of great importance!"

"I suppose it seems great to him," thought Walton. "Well," he said aloud, "you have aroused by curiosity. It is only fair to gratify it."

"That is what I propose to do. Let me say, then, that this day has made a great change in me."

"I don't see any change," said Walton, puzzled.

"Yet it has; I awoke this morning a poor man.   To-night I am rich."

"You—haven't been speculating?" said Walton, curiously.

"No; I had no money to speculate with. But to-day a fortune has come to me."

" A fortune!   How much?"

"One hundred thousand dollars!" answered the physician.

" A hundred thousand dollars!" ejaculated Nicholas Walton, staring at his brother-in-law in amazement.

"Yes."

" Explain yourself—that is, if you are not joking."

"Fortunately it is not a joke.   As to the explanation, here it is: Some years ago I was called, when a young practitioner in New York (I began here, you know), to attend a wealthy West Indian planter, boarding at the New York Hotel.   He was critically sick, and required constant attention.   I had little to do, and devoted myself to him.   He was convinced that he owed his life to me.   He paid me handsomely then, and requested me to keep him apprised of my whereabouts. I have done so. Yesterday I received a letter, requesting me to come to New York, and call at a certain room in the Fifth Avenue Hotel. I did so. I found a Cuban gentleman, who, first apprising me that my former patient was dead, added, to my amazement, that he had left me in his will one hundred thousand dollars. Furthermore, he had the amount with him in negotiable securities, and transferred them at once to my hands."

" And you have them with you?"

" Yes."

" It was strangely informal."

" True, but this gentleman was about to sail for Europe, to be absent five years—he sailed this afternoon—and he wished to be rid of his commission."

" It is like a romance," said the merchant, slowly.

" Yes, it's like a romance. I don't mind telling you," added the doctor, in a lower tone, " that it relieves me very much. Conscious, as I am, that my life hangs on a thread, it makes me easy about the future of my wife and child."

"Your life hangs on a thread? What do you mean?"

"I mean," said the physician, seriously, "that our family is subject to heart disease. My grandfather died at a minute's notice; so did my father; so, in all probability, shall I. No insurance company, knowing this, would insure me, and, till this windfall came, I was subject at times to great anxiety."

"Does your wife—my sister—know that you have received this money?" asked Walton, slowly.

"No; she merely knows that I received a letter from New York."

"And you are really liable to die suddenly?"

"Yes; I shall probably drop dead some day. My father died at my present age. Any sudden excitement——"

"Good heavens! what is the matter with you?" exclaimed Walton, springing to his feet, excitedly.

"What do you mean?" asked the physician, startled.

"Your face is livid; you look like a corpse. Great heavens! has your time come?"

Doctor Baker rose to his feet in terrible agitation; his face changed; he put his hand on his heart, swayed himself for a moment, and then fell lifeless.

Walton had supplied the sudden excitement, and brought upon him the family doom.

Nicholas Walton, half-terrified, half-triumphant, gazed at his victim. He knelt down, and tearing open the vest of his visitor, placed his hand upon his heart.

It had ceased to beat.

"Now for the securities!" he murmured hoarsely.

They were found. A brief examination showed that they were negotiable by bearer. He carefully locked them up in his desk, and then, ringing the bell hastily, summoned a physician. One came, but could afford no help.

"Now," he said to himself, with inward exultation, "this fortune is mine, and I can realize the dream of my life! No one will ever be the wiser."

CHAPTER IV.

THE MOCK PHILANTHROPIST.

NICHOLAS WALTON, much sooner than he had anticipated, was able to realize the dream of his life. He engaged a larger store on Broadway, within three months of the death of his brother-in-law. The latter was supposed to have died a poor man. In settling up his estate it was found that he left only the modest cottage in which he had lived. Mrs. Baker's anxiety, however, was alleviated by the following letter from her brother Nicholas:

"MY DEAR SISTER:—I sympathize with you sincerely in your sad and sudden loss. I am afraid my poor brother-in-law has not been able to leave you comfortably provided for. I cannot do as much as I would like, but I will send you a monthly sum of twenty-five dollars, which, as you have no rent to pay, will perhaps keep you comfortable. If I can at any time feel justified in so doing, I will increase this allowance."

"Nicholas is very kind," said Mrs. Baker, to her friends. "He has done this without any appeal from me."

She really felt grateful for his kindness, as she termed it, having no suspicion of the terrible secret that haunted her brother day and night, making him an unhappy man in spite of his outward prosperity. But he had no intention of making restitution; his remorse did not go so far as this.

"As to taking a hundred thousand dollars from my business," he said, in answer to conscience, "it would cripple me seriously. Besides, my sister doesn't want it; it would do her no good. She and her children can live comfortably on what I send her."

He tried to persuade himself that he was liberal in his provision for his sister; but even his effrontery could not go so far as this.

In reality, Mrs. Baker would have found great difficulty in keeping her expenses within three hundred dollars a year if Ben had not managed to pick up a dollar or two a week by working at odd jobs, running errands, or assisting some of the neighboring farmers. But

the small town of Sunderland did not satisfy the ambitious boy. There was no kind
of business which he could learn at home that
offered him a satisfactory career.

"Mother," he said, about three months before my story begins, "don't you think my
uncle would give me a place in his store?"

"You don't want to leave home, Ben, do
you?"

"I don't want to leave you, mother; but
you know how it is. There is nothing to do
in Sunderland."

"I am sure you pick up considerable money
in the course of a year, Ben."

"But what does it all amount to, mother?"

"It is a great help to me," said Mrs. Baker.

"I don't mean that. It isn't getting me
ahead. I can't do any more now than I could
a year ago. If I learned my uncle's business
I might get ahead, as he has."

"You may be right, Ben; but how could I
spare you? I should feel so lonely."

"You have Alice, mother. She is ten years
old, and is a good deal of company to you."

So the discussion continued. Finally, as

might have been expected, Ben obtained from his mother a reluctant consent to his writing to his uncle. He did not have to wait long for the answer ; but when it came, it was cold and unsatisfactory. It read thus :

" NEPHEW BENJAMIN :—Your letter has come to hand, asking me to give you a place in my store. I think you are much better off in the country. Besides that, I do not think you ought to leave your mother. You say there is no chance for you in Sunderland ; but you are mistaken. You can work for some farmer, and gradually acquire a knowledge of the business, and in time I may help you buy a farm, or at any rate hire one, if I am satisfied with your conduct. As to the city, you had better keep away from it. I am sure your mother will agree with me.
" Your uncle,
" NICHOLAS WALTON."

" Your uncle seems to me to write very sensibly," said Mrs. Baker. " The city is full of temptations."

" If I go to the city I shall work too hard to be troubled in that way, mother."

" Your uncle makes a very kind offer, I think."

" It doesn't bind him to much," said Ben.

"He says he may help me to buy or hire a farm, if I learn farming."

" That would be a gift worth having, Ben," said his mother, who thought chiefly of keeping Ben at home.

"I shall never make a farmer, mother; I don't like it well enough. It is a very useful and honorable business, I know, but I have a taste for business; and if Uncle Nicholas won't help me to a start, I must see what I can do for myself after a time."

Nicholas Walton congratulated himself when his letter to Ben remained unanswered.

"That will settle the matter," he said to himself. "I would rather keep the boy in the country. I couldn't have him in my establishment. I should never see him without thinking of his father's sudden death before my eyes," and the rich merchant shuddered in spite of himself. "Besides," and a shade of apprehension swept over his face, "I am in constant fear lest he should hear of the large sum of money which came into his father's hands just before his death. While he stays in Sunderland, there is little chance of any such knowledge coming to him; if he is in the city, there is a greater chance of it. Who knows; the man who paid Doctor Baker the money may turn up. It was his intention to go to Europe for five years. That period has nearly passed already. If this discovery should ever be made, I am ruined. I might even be accused of murdering him, though, happily, that could not be proved. But there would be a blot on my name, and my reputation would suffer."

For three months Ben made no sign, and his uncle concluded that he had given up his plan of coming to New York in search of employment.

But one evening—it was the one on which our story commenced—on his way back from a call upon some friends in Brooklyn, Nicholas Walton stepped into Hitchcock's lunchroom, knowing it well by reputation, and was startled by seeing the nephew whose appearance he so much dreaded.

It was his first impulse to speak to him, and harshly demand his reason for disobeying the positive command to remain at home; but this might be followed by an appeal for help (it was clear that Mr. Walton did not understand his nephew) and that might be awkward.

"No," thought the merchant; "I won't speak to him till he comes to the store, as no doubt he intends to. Then I will give him a piece of my mind."

We now come back to Ben and his new found friend, the reporter.

"If you don't object, I will walk down town with you, Mr. Manton," said Ben, as they left the restaurant where they had breakfasted.

"I shall be glad of your company, Ben," said Manton, cordially. "I will point out to you the chief landmarks, and places of interest, as we go along."

"I wish you would," said Ben. "I know very little of the city."

"That is a defect you will soon remedy," said his friend.

"By the way," said Ben, with a sudden thought, "how was it that you asked me if I knew Mr. Walton?"

"Because I saw that Mr. Walton knew you."

"You saw that he knew me?" repeated Ben, puzzled.

"Yes. Do you remember a stout gentleman who came into Hitchcock's just as we were going out?"

"No; I did not observe him."

"It was Nicholas Walton. When his glance first rested upon you he started and looked disturbed."

"He did not approve of my coming to New York," explained Ben. "Then you think he recognized me?"

"I am sure of it."

"I wonder he did not speak to me!" said Ben, thoughtfully.

"Probably for the reason you have assigned—because he did not approve of your coming. Do you expect to call upon him?"

"Yes; I am going to ask if he won't give me a place in his store. He employs a large number, I suppose?"

"Yes; not less than a hundred, I should think, in various ways inside the store, besides scores of seamstresses outside. He has a very large establishment, and is accounted a very rich man."

"So I have always heard," said Ben. "He wanted me to stay in Sunderland and become a farmer."

"And you don't fancy the advice?"

"No. I should never make a farmer. If I had any taste for it, I might have followed my uncle's advice."

"Have you ever seen Mr. Walton's store?" asked the reporter, presently.

"No."

"Here it is," and he pointed to a spacious store, with great plate-glass windows, in which was displayed suits of clothes in profusion.

"Then, Mr. Manton, I believe I will leave you and go in. I want to find out as soon as possible whether my uncle will help me, or whether I must depend upon myself."

"Good luck to you, Ben, then! I will expect to see you to-night."

And Hugh Manton kept on his way down town, to see what work had been laid out for him at the office.

CHAPTER V.

A YOUNG DUDE.

BEN entered the great store, gazing not without admiration at the long counters loaded with piles of clothing.

"My uncle must be a very rich man," he said to himself. "Surely he can find a place for me in so large a store."

"Do you wish to buy a suit?" asked a spruce young man, coming forward to meet our hero.

"No; I would like to see Mr. Walton," answered Ben.

The young man surveyed Ben's country garb with a smile of depreciation. He was apt to judge others by their clothes, being conscious, perhaps, that they were his own chief claim to consideration.

"I don't think Mr. Walton will see you, youngster," he said.

" Why not?" demanded Ben, looking him calmly in the eye.

" His time is of too much value to waste on country kids."

" Mr. Walton is my uncle," said Ben, quietly.

" Your uncle!" repeated the clerk, in considerable surprise. " Oh, well, that alters the case. Just go through the store and you will find Mr. Walton in his office."

Ben followed directions, and found the office without further inquiry.

Through the open door he saw a short man, of fifty or thereabouts, sitting at a desk. There was another person in the office—a boy, somewhere near his own age—dressed in the fashion, with a gold watch-chain across his vest, a showy pin in his scarf, and the air of a young coxcomb.

This was Clarence Plantagenet Walton, the only son of the merchant, and of course Ben's cousin. The two, however, had not met since both were very young boys, and neither would have recognized the other.

Ben overheard a fragment of the conversation between his uncle and cousin.

"You spend too much money, Plantagenet. It is less than a week since I gave you ten dollars."

"The fellows I go with are all rich, and spend plenty of money. You wouldn't want them to look upon me as mean, pa?"

"The boys of the present day are altogether too extravagant," said his father, frowning. "Why, when I was a boy, I didn't spend ten dollars in three months."

"You were not in fashionable society like me, pa," said Clarence Plantagenet, consequentially.

"Much good it does you!" muttered Mr. Walton. "What do you want money for particularly to-day?"

"I am going with Percy Van Dyke to a base-ball match this afternoon. Percy lives in a splendid house on Fifth avenue, and his family is one of the first. I suppose we shall get home late, and I want to give him a little supper at Delmonico's."

"The Van Dykes stand very high," said Mr. Walton, complacently. "I am very glad to have you associate with such a high-toned family. I suppose I must let you have the money."

He drew out a ten-dollar bill and tendered it to Clarence.

"Five dollars more, if you please, pa," said the elegant youth. "Suppers at Delmonico's are expensive, and I don't want to economize with such a fellow as Percy."

"Very well; here are five dollars more, but don't be foolishly extravagant."

Clarence was about to leave the office, well satisfied, when he espied Ben.

"Who do you want to see, boy?" he demanded, curtly.

"I should like to speak with my uncle," answered Ben.

"Then don't hang around my father's office. If your uncle is employed in this establishment, you can ask one of the floor-walkers to point him out."

Ben eyed the arrogant boy in some amusement, and answered, demurely:

"My uncle is Mr. Nicholas Walton, and you, I suppose, are my cousin Clarence."

Clarence Plantagenet recoiled in disgust.

"I don't understand you," he said. "You must be crazy."

Ben was not obliged to vindicate his sanity, for his uncle, who had hitherto remained silent, now spoke.

"You can come in, if you are Benjamin Baker, of Sunderland."

"Thank you, Uncle Nicholas," said Ben.

"Is he my cousin?" asked Plantagenet of his father, in evident discomposure.

"Yes, I presume so. His mother is my sister."

"Did you send for him, pa?"

"No."

"Then why is he here?"

"I expect him to explain that to me," said Mr. Walton, coldly. "Benjamin, what brings you to New York?"

"I want to get a position here, so that I may learn business. I thought you might find me a place in your store, Uncle Nicholas."

"Did I not write you to stay in Sunderland?" asked Mr. Walton, coldly.

"Yes."

" Then why have you disobeyed me ?" continued the merchant, with a frown.

" Because I have no taste for farming, and
there is no other employment there."

" A boy like you is not qualified to judge
what is best for him," said Mr. Walton,
harshly. " Did I not promise, if you learned
farming, that when you got older I would set
you up on a farm of your own ?"

" I never should succeed as a farmer, for I
don't like it," answered Ben.

" What fault have you to find with it?" demanded the merchant, testily.

" None whatever, uncle, except that I am
not suited for it."

" You don't look to me suited for anything
else," said Clarence Plantagenet, insolently.

"I don't think you know me well enough to
judge what I am fit for," answered Ben, calmly.

" You might make a good blacksmith, perhaps," continued Clarence, in the same offen-
sive tone. " Isn't there any opening in that
line in the country ?"

" There might be. The business is not to
my taste, though it may be to yours."

"To my taste!" ejaculated the horrified Plantagenet. "What have I to do with such a dirty business as that?"

"Stop this foolish discussion, Plantagenet," said his father. "You had better go to meet your friend, Van Dyke, and I will settle matters with your cousin here."

"Pack him back to the country, pa!" said Clarence. "That is the best place for him."

So saying, the young "dude" sauntered out out of the office and left the store, several of the clerks who wished to stand well with their employer bowing deferentially to him. Plantagenet barely acknowledged their bows by a supercilious nod. He did not look upon them as his social equals.

"I am inclined to agree with my son," said the merchant, after Plantagenet had left the office. "I think the country is the best place for you."

"Then, Uncle Nicholas, you won't give me a place in your store?" asked Ben, his face showing his disappointment.

"I will do nothing to encourage you in a

step which I consider so ill-advised as coming to the city."

"Then I must bid you good-morning," said Ben, soberly.

"Stay !" said his uncle. "I am willing to make up to you the expense of your trip to the city, on condition that you go back to-day."

He put his hand into his pocket as he spoke.

"Thank you, Uncle Nicholas," said Ben. "I thank you for your offer, but I won't accept it; I shall not go back to Sunderland."

"You won't go back !" gasped the merchant. "What will you do, then ?"

"Look elsewhere for a place," said Ben.

"You are a foolish, headstrong boy. I wash my hands of you. You need not expect any help from me. You must make your own way."

"I mean to," answered Ben, quietly, as he bowed and walked out of the office.

"This is very annoying," said Mr. Walton to himself. "He is an obstinate boy. However, his eyes will soon be opened to his folly, and he will have to go back, after all. Perhaps it is as well for him to try, and fail. He will be more manageable afterward."

CHAPTER VI.

BEN GETS INTO TROUBLE.

BEN went out of his uncle's store in a serious frame of mind. He knew that his uncle was opposed to his leaving his country home and coming to New York, but he had hoped that he would nevertheless be willing to extend to him a helping hand, especially as it would cost him so little.

He found himself now in a critical position He had in his pocket a dollar and twenty-seven cents, and this constituted his entire worldly capital. It was enough to carry him back to Sunderland, but, if he had been willing to do that, it would have been for his interest to accept his uncle's offer to refund to him what his trip would cost.

But Ben was not easily discouraged. His motto was:

> " If at first you don't succeed,
> Try, try again !"

"I won't go back to Sunderland unless I am obliged to," he said to himself. "There are other stores besides my uncle's in this large city, and more ways of making a living than one. I won't give up till I have tried my best."

So he walked along Broadway in a leisurely way, keeping his eyes wide open, and interested, in spite of his critical circumstances, in the crowds and bustle of that brilliant thoroughfare.

Presently he came to a shop window on which was posted the notice—

"Boy Wanted."

"Here's a chance for me," he thought, hopefully. "I'll apply for the place. I can't be any more than refused."

He entered. It was a store appropriated to "Gentlemen's Furnishing Goods."

A tall young man, with his auburn hair parted in the middle, glanced at him languidly.

"I see you want a boy," said Ben, plunging at once into business.

"Humph! Are you the boy?"

"I am a boy, and would like a place," answered Ben.

The clerk picked his teeth languidly with a wooden toothpick which he had brought from the cheap restaurant where he had taken his breakfast.

" Are you from the country ?"

" Yes, sir."

" How long have you been in the city ?"

" I arrived yesterday."

" Then you don't know your way round New York ?"

" No; but I would soon learn."

" That wouldn't suit us. Besides, you don't live with your parents."

" My father is dead; my mother lives in the country."

" You won't suit us, then. However, you can go back and speak to Mr. Talbot. There he is, in the rear of the store."

Ben had at first supposed that the young man with whom he was speaking was the proprietor. He did not dream that he was a clerk, working for nine dollars a week. He made application to Mr. Talbot, a middle-aged gentleman, not half so consequential as his clerk, but was asked essentially the same questions as before.

"I am afraid I must refuse you," said Mr. Talbot, kindly. "We require a boy who is used to the city streets, and we prefer that he should live with his parents. I am sorry for your disappointment."

"Thank you, sir," said Ben; but it was in rather a subdued tone. His prospects did not seem quite so good as a little while before.

Coming out into the street, Ben saw quite a crowd of boys and young men, who were following a tall lady, just in advance, and showing signs of amusement. It only took a glance to discover the cause of their mirth.

The lady wore a sack, evidently just purchased, on which was a card, bearing in large, distinct characters, the words:

"CHEAP FOR CASH."

This it was that had excited the amusement of the crowd.

Ben was also amused, but he sympathized

with the lady; and, stepping forward promptly, touched her on the arm.

She looked back in surprise, and then for
the first time became aware of the crowd that
was following her. She was a lady probably
nearing forty, and had a shrewd, kindly look.

"What does it all mean?" she asked.

"There is something on your sack, madam.
Allow me to remove it."

And Ben plucked off the ticket, which he
handed to the lady.

"I am not surprised at the amusement of
the boys," said the lady, smiling. "The
ticket should have been removed. I am very
much obliged to you, my young friend."

"You are quite welcome," said Ben, bowing and falling back.

The lady smiled, and passed on. She
would have remained had she known that by
his act of kindness her young acquaintance
had involved himself in trouble.

No sooner had the lady disappeared than
the disappointed young ruffians who had been
making sport of her turned angrily upon our
hero.

"Ain't you smart?" sneered one.

"You're a little too fresh, country!" said another.

Ben turned from one to another in surprise. He didn't understand in what way he had offended.

"What is the matter?" he asked.   "What have I done?"

"What made you tell the lady what she had on her back?" demanded a third.

"I thought she ought to know," answered Ben.

"Oh, you did!" sneered the first.   "What you wanted was a reward.   I'm glad she didn't give you a cent."

"You judge me by yourself," said Ben, provoked.   "I can be polite without being paid for it."

"Say that again!" said Mike Rafferty, a freckle-faced young rowdy, squaring off in a scientific manner.

"All right; I do say it again!" returned Ben, angrily.

"Take that, then!" said the fellow, as he struck at Ben.

Our hero dodged, and returned the compliment.

At that moment a policeman came round the corner, just in time to see Ben's demonstration.

"So you're fightin' agin, you young rascal!" exclaimed the valiant officer. "I've got ye this time!" and he seized Ben by the shoulder.

Ben turned, and, it must be confessed, was startled to find himself, for the first time in his life, in the hands of the law.

"That boy attacked me, sir," he said.

"It's a lie!" exclaimed Mike Rafferty, "Isn't it b'yes?"

"Yes, it's a lie!" chimed in his companions, whose sympathies, of course, were with Mike.

"Jist what I thought meself," said the astute officer.

"Say, cop, ye didn't see me hit him?" said Mike.

"Don't ye call me cop!" said the policeman, with insulted dignity.

"I mean captain," amended Mike, craftily.

"What's all the fuss about?" interrogated the officer.

"I axed him was he from the country, and he got mad and hit me," said Mike. "Say, b'yes, ain't it so?"

"Yes, that's so," answered the boys, in chorus.

"Then you must come with me, you young rascal!" said the officer.

"Where?" asked Ben, with sinking heart.

"To the station-house. I'll tache ye to fight in the streets. You must go along, too, and make complaint," he added, addressing Mike Rafferty.

"All right, captain. Come along, b'yes," said Mike, with a wink of enjoyment at his companions.

Ben felt not a little humiliated at walking along Broadway in the clutch of a policeman. He felt bewildered, too, it had come upon him so quickly. It really seemed as if misfortunes were crowding upon him. First, his uncle had practically disowned him, he had been rebuffed in his attempt to obtained employment, and now he was arrested, and on his way to the station-house, charged with fighting and disorderly conduct in the streets.

To make matters worse and heighten his humiliation, as he was walking along, shrinking from observation, he met his cousin, Clarence Plantagenet, in company with another boy, somewhat older, dressed also in the height of the fashion.

Clarence regarded Ben in amazement, and turned away his head in a disgust which he did not attempt to conceal.

" He will tell Uncle Nicholas," thought our unfortunate hero, " and he will think I have been doing something disgraceful."

" Come along, ye young rapscallion !" said the policeman, roughly, "I'll soon attind to your case."

CHAPTER VII.

A STRANGE ADVENTURE.

UNDER different circumstances Ben might have been interested in his first view of a police station. But, standing before the bar in the custody of a policeman, he felt too much troubled in mind to notice his surroundings. As another prisoner was under examination, fifteen minutes elapsed before Ben's turn came.

"What is the charge against this boy?" asked the sergeant.

"I caught him fightin' in the streets," said the officer. "He was hittin' that b'ye yonder," indicating Mike Rafferty.

Mike, who looked emphatically like a hard case, tried to appear like a respectable, well-behaved boy, who had been set upon by a young ruffian.

"What's your name?" asked the sergeant, addressing Mike.

"Mike Rafferty, yer honor," answered Mike, thinking it best to be as respectable as possible.

"Did this boy strike you?"

"Yes, and he did, your honor, and if you don't believe me just ax any of them b'yes," indicating his companions. "Tommy Burke, didn't you see him hit me?"

"That will do. What did he hit you for?"

"Faith, and I don't know," said Mike, shrugging his shoulders.

"Did you hit him first?"

"No, I didn't do nothing to him," answered Mike, virtuously.

"I think you have been here before," said the sergeant, whose memory was good.

"I don't remember it," said Mike, cautiously, not thinking it politic to contradict the sergeant.

"Officer, do you know anything of the boy you have brought in?"

"Oh, yes, I've known him a long time. He's wan of the gang," answered the policeman, glibly.

Just then a gentleman came forward, whom, much to Ben's delight, he remembered as the keeper of a dry-goods store in Sunderland. Bowing to the sergeant, he said, respectfully:

"I know this boy, and I know that the policeman is under a great mistake. Will you allow me to say what I know about him?"

"Go on, sir."

"So far from his being a member of any city gang, he lives in the country, and it is extremely doubtful if the policeman ever saw him before. He only came to the city yesterday."

"He's wan of the gang," persisted the officer, sullenly. "I've seen him ivery day for the last three months."

"Mr. Sergeant," said the former speaker, "this officer is guilty of willful falsehood. I know the boy as well as I know my own son, and I know that he has passed the last three months in the country."

"The boy is discharged," said the officer. He added, sharply: "Officer Flynn, I expect the truth from you in future. The boy you have arrested is much more respectable in appearance than his accuser, and, under the circumstances, I cannot attach any credit to your charge against him. Be more careful in future."

With sullen reluctance, the officer, who is a type of a considerable number on the force, but not of all, released Ben.

Our hero walked up to the gentleman whose testimony had been of so much value to him, and warmly thanked him.

"I was in a bad scrape," he said, "and I don't know how I would have come out of it if you had not spoken for me."

"I chanced to see you in charge, and followed as soon as I could," said Mr. Woodbury. "What luck are you meeting with in New York, Ben?"

"Not much, yet; but don't say anything to mother about your meeting me here, or she may be worried. I shall make every effort to get something to do here. If I can't, I may be obliged to go home."

"Well, Ben, I wish you good luck. I must now leave you, as I have several business calls to make."

Ben emerged from the station-house feeling that he had made a lucky escape. The boys who had followed him (Mike and his friends) had vanished, on finding that things did not turn out as they expected, fearing that they might get into trouble themselves.

"I see," said Ben to himself, "that I must keep my eyes wide open in New York. I used to think that an innocent person need not fear the police, but I don't find it exactly so."

He strolled back to Broadway, and mingled once more with the busy crowds. The same thought came to him, as to so many in his position, "Everybody seems to have something to do except me. Why am I alone idle?"

When Ben reached the Metropolitan Hotel he paused for a moment at the entrance. As he stood there a gentleman passed out hurriedly. As his eyes fell upon Ben his face lighted up, and a sudden plan presented itself to his mind.

"Boy," he said, "do you live in New York?"

"I expect to, if I can find anything to do."

"Where do you come from?"

" Sunderland."

" Where is that ?"

" In Connecticut."

" How far away is it ?"

" About forty miles."

" What relatives have you living ?"

" A mother and sister in the country."

As the gentleman did not inquire whether he had relatives in New York, Ben did not see fit to volunteer information, particularly as he did not care to claim relationship with an uncle and cousin who were evidently ashamed of him.

"You are in search of a position, are you?" asked the gentleman.

" Yes, sir."

"And you are not particular what you do?"

" No, sir, as long as it is honest."

" Yes, I think he will do," soliloquized the gentleman, regarding Ben intently. " He is the same size and shape, and has a similar expression. It will be easy to mistake him for Philip."

Ben only caught part of this soliloquy, and of course he did not understand it.

"Of course, of course," said the gentleman, hastily, answering Ben's words after a while. "Well, I think I can give you something to do. Do you write a fair hand?"

"Yes, sir, pretty fair."

"Come up stairs with me," said the gentleman, abruptly. "I am staying at this hotel."

"Is it safe?" thought Ben; but the thought that he was a poor boy, and was little likely to attract the attention of adventurers, reassured him, and without hesitation he followed his new, and, as it appeared, rather eccentric acquaintance.

They took the elevator and got out at the fourth landing.

His new friend nodded, and Ben followed him along the hall.

The gentleman drew a key from his pocket and opened the door of a room near at hand.

"Come in," he said.

The room was a double one, consisting of a parlor and bedchamber. There were two trunks in the bedroom.

"Sit down," said the gentleman.

Ben seated himself.

· " What is your name ?"

" Benjamin Baker."

" I engage you as my private secretary."

" Do you think I will suit ?" asked Ben, considerably amazed.

" You won't have much to do," was the answer. " You are also to pass for my nephew."

" I wonder whether I am awake or dreaming," he asked himself.

" I shall call you Philip Grafton," continued the stranger.

" Why can't I keep my own name ?" asked Ben, uneasily.

" It is unnecessary to state. My secretary must be Philip Grafton," said the gentleman, firmly. " Don't you like the name ?"

" Yes, sir; it is a good name. Many would prefer it to mine, but I don't like to sail under false colors."

" It is a whim of mine," said the gentleman, " but I don't think you will be sorry for acceding to it. Now, as to compensation, I propose to pay you fifty dollars a month and board—that is, of course, you will live with me."

"Fifty dollars a month!" repeated Ben, opening his eyes in amazement.

"Yes; isn't it satisfactory?"

"I don't see how I can possibly earn fifty dollars a month."

"That is my lookout. As long as I am satisfied, you needn't worry about that."

"I am afraid you will be disappointed in me, sir."

"I hope not. Do as I tell you, and I shall be satisfied."

"When am I to go to work?" asked Ben.

"You will enter upon your duties at once. I suppose you have no objection?"

"Am I to live at the hotel with you, sir?"

"Yes."

"Then I will go and get my clothes."

"Ah, yes; I didn't think of that. You won't need to get them."

"Won't need to get my clothes?" repeated Ben in amazement.

He began to think his employer was out of his head.

"I have clothes for you here—in that trunk. This key fits it. Open it."

Wondering much, Ben took the key, and, fitting it in the lock of the smaller trunk, lifted the lid. He found it full of shirts, under-garments, handkerchiefs, etc., of fine texture.

"You will find underneath two suits of clothes," said his employer. "Take them out."

Ben followed directions.

"Now take off your own clothes—all of them —and dress yourself from the contents of the trunk."

Ben hesitated. He could not at all under-stand what was happening to him.

"Of course," said the gentleman, "your present clothing won't do for my private sec-retary. The contents of this trunk are yours, if the clothes fit you."

Ben proceeded to remove his clothing, and in a few minutes he was newly rigged from top to toe. Every article fitted admirably.

"Now look at yourself in the mirror," said the gentleman, evidently pleased with the transformation.

Ben looked in the mirror, and was delighted with the change in his appearance. His outer suit was of fine French cloth, all his under-garments were of costly fabric, and he found himself transformed from a country boy in badly-cut garments of coarse cloth to a finely-dressed young gentleman.

" How do you like it?" asked the gentleman, smiling.

" Very much," said Ben, sincerely.

" So do I," answered the gentleman.

" Where shall I put my old clothes?" asked Ben.

" Make a bundle of them and give them to some poor boy. You won't need them."

Ben resolved, instead, to send them home by express. They might come in use some time.

" Now," said the gentleman, " there is one thing more. Have you a pocket-book?"

" Yes, sir."

" Here is a little money in advance. You will need to carry some about with you."

He took from his own pocket-book fifteen dollars in bills and handed them to Ben.

" I wonder if I am dreaming," thought our hero. " This may be like the fairy gold I have read of."

As a matter of fact, however, they were bank-notes on the Park Bank of New York, and Ben soon had occasion to test their genuineness.

"We will go down to lunch now," said Richard Grafton, for that was the name of the gentleman, as Ben discovered.

Ben entered the large dining-room and took a seat next his employer. Though new to hotel life he copied what he saw other guests do, and no one suspected that the handsomely-dressed boy had not all his life been used to luxury.

When the meal was over, Mr. Grafton said:

"You can go where you please this after-noon, but be on hand at six o'clock. We shall go to some theatre this evening."

Mr. Grafton left the hotel. Ben took an opportunity to examine the hotel register soon after. He discovered that Mr. Grafton had arrived the day before.

This was the entry:

"RICHARD GRAFTON, London, England."

Underneath, to his amazement, he read an-other name:

"MASTER PHILIP GRAFTON, London, England."

"I suppose that means me," he said to himself. "What does it all mean? How did Mr. Grafton know that I would be here? He had never seen me. And how did he find clothes to fit me so exactly?"

There was certainly a mystery, but it was fraught with so much to the advantage of our hero that he resolved to cease asking questions and accept the gifts of fortune.

CHAPTER VIII.

AN UNEXPECTED MEETING AT THE GRAND OPERA HOUSE.

WHEN Clarence Plantagenet saw his poor country cousin marching up Broadway escorted by a policeman he was very much surprised, but on the whole he was not displeased.

"Do you know that boy?" asked his companion.

"No, certainly not," answered Clarence, coloring.

"I thought you looked as if you did."

"He looks like a boy I met in the country last summer," was the evasive answer.

"Poor devil! I wonder what he has been doing."

"Stealing, very likely," said Clarence, shrugging his shoulders.

"He doesn't look like a thief."

"Appearances are deceitful," said Clarence, oracularly.

At the supper-table, where Clarence met his father for the first time since he had called at his office, he said:

"Oh, papa, what do you think? That country boy I saw in your office has got into trouble."

"Do you mean your cousin Benjamin?"

"I suppose he is my cousin," said Clarence, reluctantly, "but I don't care about knowing him for a relation. I saw him on Broadway in charge of a policeman."

"Are you sure of this?" said Mr. Walton, much surprised.

"Yes; I knew him well enough by his clothes."

Clarence then gave an account of his meeting Ben.

"Did you speak to him?" asked his father.

"Mercy, no! Percy Van Dyke was with me. I wouldn't for a hundred dollars have him know that I had a cousin arrested, and such a countryfied-looking cousin, too."

"I think Benjamin would be a good-looking boy if he were well dressed," said Mr. Walton.

"I don't," said Clarence, decidedly.

"I am sorry to hear he has got into trouble," said Mr. Walton, who was not so mean as his son. "I think I ought to do something to help him."

"Better leave him to his fate, pa. No doubt he is a bad boy."

"I can't understand why he should be. My sister is poor but an excellent woman, and his father was an exemplary man."

"I don't think we have any call to trouble ourselves about this boy," said Clarence. "He has disgraced us, and we couldn't do anything without having it all come out."

"By the way, Clarence, I have two tickets to the Grand Opera House this evening; would you like to go?"

"Just the thing, pa; I was wondering what we should do to pass the time."

"Edwin Booth is to appear as Cardinal Richelieu. It is one of his best characters. It will be a rare treat."

"Percy Van Dyke is to be there with his

sister," said Clarence. "That is the reason why he wouldn't take supper with me at Delmonico's this evening."

"You will have a chance to see your friends between the acts," said Mr. Walton. "I am perfectly willing you should become intimate with the Van Dykes. By the way, bring your friend around and introduce him to me."

"Yes, pa."

Mr. Walton had been the architect of his own fortune, while the Van Dykes were descended from an old Dutch family, and had held for over a century a high social position. Now that the merchant had money, he thirsted for social recognition—something money will not always buy.

Eight o'clock found father and son in choice orchestra seats in the Grand Opera House, and they began to look about them.

Suddenly Mr. Walton said, sharply:

"What was all that rubbish you were telling me about your cousin being arrested?"

"It was perfectly true, pa," answered Clarence, looking at his father in surprise.

" What do you say to that, then ?"

Following the direction of his father's finger, Clarence's eyes rested upon his despised
country cousin, elegantly dressed, sitting two
rows to the front, and a little to the right,
with his eyes fixed upon the curtain, which
was then rising.

"That looks very much as if your cousin had
been arrested!" said his father, with a sneer.

"I can't understand it," ejaculated Clarence. "It can't be my cousin. It must be
some other boy that looks like him."

Just then Ben chanced to turn round.
Observing his uncle's eyes fixed upon him,
he bowed politely and turned once more to
the stage.

CHAPTER IX.

CLARENCE IS PUZZLED.

CLARENCE PLANTAGENET was so puzzled by the appearance of his cousin at a fashionable theatre at a time when he supposed him to be enjoying the hospitality of the police authorities that he paid little attention to the stage performance. He had a large share of curiosity, and resolved to gratify it, even if it were necessary to speak to Ben himself.

At the end of the second act, Ben, feeling thirsty, and having noticed that ice-water could be obtained in the lobby, left his seat and walked up the aisle.

Clarence, observing this, rose also, and followed him.

He came to the water-fount just as Ben had quenched his thirst. He was surprised anew when he observed how elegantly his cousin was dressed. He was fastidious as to his own dress, but was obliged to confess that Ben surpassed him in this respect.

Ben was conscious of the same thing, and, under the circumstances, it gratified him.

Another thing also was evident to Clarence, though he admitted it with reluctance, that Ben was a strikingly handsome boy. He had appeared somewhat to disadvantage in his country-made suit, but all signs of rusticity had now disappeared.

"Good evening," said Clarence, with a good deal more politeness than he had displayed at the office.

"Good evening," said Ben, politely.

"I am surprised to see you here," continued Clarence.

"Yes," answered Ben. "I didn't expect to see you here."

"Oh, I come here often. I thought you would spend the evening in an entirely different place," said Clarence, significantly.

"You are kind to think of me at all," said Ben, smiling.

Clarence was puzzled. He began to think

that he must have been mistaken in the person when he supposed he saw Ben in the custody of an officer. Now he came to think of it, the boy under arrest had shown no signs of recognition. We know that it was because Ben was far from wishing to attract the attention of any one who knew him.

"Have you passed the day pleasantly?" inquired Clarence, thinking he might lead up to the subject on which he desired light.

"Quite pleasantly," answered Ben. "New York is a beautiful city."

"I was afraid you had got into a scrape," said Clarence. "As I was walking along Broadway, soon after you left father's office, I saw a boy just like you in charge of a policeman."

"Poor fellow! I hope he got off. Did you stop and speak to him?"

"No; I was so surprised that I stood still and stared till it was too late."

"I am not at all anxious to make the acquaintance of the police," said Ben, not sorry to have put his cousin off the scent.

"You have changed your dress," said

Clarence, wishing to satisfy his curiosity in another direction.

"Yes," answered Ben, with studied indifference.

"You have a good seat to-night."

"Yes; I have an excellent view of the play."

"The orchestra seats are high-priced. I thought you were short of money."

"I was, but I am earning a good income now, and——"

"You haven't got a place, have you?" ejaculated his cousin, in surprise.

"Yes, I have."

"Is it in a store?"

"No; I am private secretary to a gentleman living at the Metropolitan Hotel."

"Private secretary!" exclaimed Clarence, in continued surprise. "You can't be fit for such a position. How did you get it?"

"I am not sure whether I shall suit," said Ben, "but the gentleman applied to me, and I accepted."

"I never heard of anything so strange. How much pay do you get?"

"Fifty dollars a month and board."

"It can't be possible!"

"That is what I say to myself," responded Ben, good-naturedly. "I am afraid that my employer will find out that he is paying me too much money."

"Are you staying at the Metropolitan, too?"

"Yes, for the present."

"I will call on you before long."

"Thank you."

"My aristocratic cousin seems disposed to be very polite to me now," thought Ben. "I am glad I put him off the track about the arrest."

"Excuse me," he said. "I believe the curtain is rising."

"Who is that fine-looking boy you were just speaking to?" asked Percy Van Dyke, who came up at this moment.

"It is a cousin of mine," answered Clarence, not unwillingly.

"I should like to know what tailor he employs. He is finely dressed, and a handsome fellow, besides."

"Of course, being a cousin of mine," said Clarence, with a smirk.

"How does it happen I have never met your cousin before?"

"He has only recently come to the city. He is staying at the Metropolitan just at present."

Wonders will never cease. Here was Clarence Plantagenet Walton, the son of a wealthy merchant, actually acknowledging with complacency his relationship to a country cousin whom earlier in the day he had snubbed.

He did not have another chance to speak to Ben that evening, as his cousin remained in his seat till the close of the performance, and in the throng at the close he lost sight of him.

As he and his father were walking home, Clarence said:

"I saw Ben in the lobby, between the acts."

"What did he say?" asked the merchant, who was himself not without curiosity.

"I must have been mistaken about his being in charge of a policeman," said Clarence.

"I thought you were."

"But the boy I saw looked precisely like Ben."

"What did your cousin say?"

"He has had a stroke of good luck. He has been engaged as private secretary to a gentleman staying at the Metropolitan Hotel."

"Is this true, Clarence?"

"So Ben says; and he says, also, that he is to receive fifty dollars a month."

"He can't be fitted for any such position with his country education."

"So I told him."

"And what did he say?"

"He agreed with me. He said he was afraid his employer would find out that he was paying him too much."

"The boy is candid. If all this is true, he is strangely lucky."

"Did you notice how stylishly he was dressed, pa?"

"I observed that he was dressed a good deal better than when he called at my office to-day."

"Even Percy Van Dyke noticed it, and asked me who he was."

"Did you tell him?"

" Yes, I said he was a cousin of mine, who was staying at the Metropolitan. He wanted to find out who was Ben's tailor."

"Your cousin seems a very smart boy. Perhaps he was right in thinking that he would be better off in the city."

"I never saw such a change in a boy in my life. I told him I would call on him at the hotel."

" Do so, Clarence. I confess I have a curiosity to learn how he has managed to get such a position."

Certainly this had been a day of strange vicissitudes to Ben. He had been in the depths of humiliation and at the summit of joy.

He had come to the city in the morning, a poor country boy. In the evening he had attended a performance at a fashionable theatre as elegantly dressed as any of his own age in the audience.

Mr. Grafton's room contained two beds, a large and a small one. The latter was appropriated to Ben.

Our hero was very tired, and Mr. Grafton was obliged to call him the next morning.

"Wake up, my boy," he said; "it is half-past eight."

"Half-past eight! Why, I got up at half-past six in the country."

"Dress yourself and we will go down to breakfast. Afterward I have to make a business call, and you must go with me."

CHAPTER X.

AT THE OFFICE OF MR. CODICIL.

IN one of the large business buildings appropriated chiefly to offices, within a stone's throw of Printing-House Square, were the commodious offices of Nathan Codicil, a prominent lawyer, whose business related chiefly to the estates of wealthy clients.

Mr. Codicil himself was a dignified-looking gentleman, of grave aspect, whose whitening locks seemed to indicate that he had reached the age of threescore. He was a cautious, careful, trustworthy man, whose reputation was deservedly high.

Mr. Grafton and Ben, stepping out of the elevator, paused before the door of Mr. Codicil's office for a moment, when the former opened the door and entered.

"You may sit down here, Philip, while I go in and speak to Mr. Codicil," said Mr. Grafton, indicating a chair near the door.

6

"I wish he wouldn't call me Philip," thought Ben. "I like my own name much better."

He did not complain aloud, however, for he felt that his salary was liberal enough to compensate him for some slight sacrifice of feeling.

"Good morning, Mr. Grafton," said the lawyer, advancing to meet his visitor.

"Good morning, Mr. Codicil; I am glad to find you in, for I've made quite an effort to reach your office at an early hour. You observe I have brought the boy with me."

The sharp eyes of the lawyer had not failed to note the presence of Ben.

"You observe that he is in excellent health, despite all reports to the contrary."

"So it appears," said the lawyer. "He seems to have lost all resemblance to the family."

"Do you think so?" said Grafton, carelessly. "Opinions differ about that. For my own part, I can see the resemblance plainly."

"How old is he now?"

"Sixteen."

"I have not seen him since he was four years of age."

"Twelve years effect many changes."

"Very true."

"And now, Mr. Codicil, as I have another engagement very soon, if you can conveniently attend to our little business at once—"

"Certainly, sir."

Mr. Codicil prepared a receipt which he requested Mr. Grafton to sign. He then opened a check-book and filled a check for a large amount, which he handed to his visitor. The latter pocketed it with evident satisfaction.

"I hope, Mr. Codicil, you are not disappointed to know that the boy is still alive?" he said.

"Heaven knows that I wish no harm to the lad!" said the lawyer, warmly. "Yet, when I consider how his poor cousins are compelled to struggle for a living, I cannot help regretting the injustice of old John Portland's will, which maintains one grandchild in luxury, while three others, having equal natural claims, should be thrown on the cold mercies of the world."

"Yes, to be sure!" said Richard Grafton, carelessly. "Still a man's last will and testament must be respected. A man can do as he likes with his own."

"True, in the eyes of the law. Morally, there would be no harm in your young ward doing something for his poor cousins. They would like to meet him and make his acquaintance."

"I am afraid it won't be possible. We remain in the city but a short time," said Mr. Grafton, hastily.

"Where do you go?"

"I have not quite decided whether to take a trip to the Pacific coast or to return to Europe. Of course I shall apprise you promptly when I have made my decision."

"Your ward is an American. Is it right to rear him in Europe, leaving him without any adequate knowledge of his own country?"

"He will have advantages abroad which he would not have in his own country. However, I will consider what you have said, and I may arrange to spend a part of each year in America."

"I would like to speak to Philip," said Mr. Codicil.

Richard Grafton hesitated, but only for a moment. He was playing a bold game for a large stake. It would not do to be timid.

"Come here, Philip," he said, "Mr. Codicil wishes to speak to you."

Ben rose and advanced to meet the lawyer.

"I am glad to make your acquaintance, sir," he said.

"And I am pleased to meet you, my boy. You look well!"

"Yes, sir; I always enjoy good health."

Mr. Codicil looked a little surprised, but he regarded with approval the boy's bright face and manly figure.

"He is certainly a very attractive boy," thought the lawyer. "I haven't much confidence in his guardian, but the boy doesn't appear to be spoiled."

"Come, Philip. I am afraid I must hurry you away," said Mr. Grafton, "as I have another visit to pay."

Ben shook hands with the lawyer and went out of his office.

"I cannot help distrusting that man," said Mr. Codicil, as the door closed. "I believe him to be a trickster. I wish the boy were under better influences."

Ben had been at such a distance from the inner office that he had not heard or understood the conversation between his employer and Mr. Codicil, yet it seemed to him singular that he should have received so much attention from the lawyer.

"I suppose Mr. Grafton was speaking to him about me," said he to himself.

When they reached the street Mr. Grafton said:

"Philip, I shall not require your company any longer this morning. If you have any plans of your own you are quite at liberty to follow them. Have you all the money you need?"

"Yes, sir; you gave me fifteen dollars yesterday."

"I remember. Very well; you can go where you please. We will meet at the hotel at one o'clock."

"Would you object, Mr. Grafton, to my

sending five dollars to my mother? I shall have enough left for myself."

"Do as you like. You may send ten dollars if you like. When you are out of money you have only to apply to me."

"You are very kind, sir," said Ben, gratefully.

"It is on account of your first month's wages, you know."

Then he paused a moment, regarding Ben with some apparent solicitude.

"By the way," he said, "I must guard you against saying too much about me or your relation with me. I have a great dislike to have myself or my affairs talked about."

"I will remember, sir."

"You need not mention that I have desired you to bear a different name from your own."

"I will not mention it, sir, if you object."

"With me it is a matter of sentiment," said Mr. Grafton in a low voice. "I had a dear son named Philip. He died, and left me alone in the world. You resemble him. It is pleasant to me to call some one by his name, yet I cannot bear to excite the curiosity of a cold, unsympathizing world, and be forced to make to them an explanation which will harrow up my feelings and recall to me my bitter loss."

"I quite understand you, Mr. Grafton," said Ben, with quiet sympathy. "Though I would prefer to be called by my own name, I am glad if I can help make up to you for your loss."

"Enough, my boy! I felt that I had judged you aright. Now go where you please. Only try to be back at the hotel at one o'clock."

As Ben walked away Richard Grafton said to himself, in a tone of self-congratulation:

"I might have sought far and wide without finding a boy that would suit my purpose as well as this one. Codicil, as shrewd as he thinks himself, was quite taken in. I confess I looked forward to the interview with dread. Had I allowed the boy to be closely questioned all would have come out, and I would have lost the handsome income which I receive as his guardian. While the real Philip

Grafton sleeps in his foreign grave, his substitute will answer my purpose, and insure me ease and. comfort. But it won't do to remain in New York. There are too many chances of discovery. I must put the sea between me and the lynx-eyed sharpness of old Codicil."

Mr. Grafton's urgent business engagement was at the Park Bank, where he got his check cashed. He next proceeded to the office of the Cunard Steamship Company, and engaged passage for the next Saturday for Richard Grafton and Master Philip Grafton.

CHAPTER XI.

THE HOME OF POVERTY.

THE time has come to introduce some new characters, who will play a part in my story.

Five minutes' walk from Bleecker street, in a tall, shabby tenement house, divided, as the custom is, into suites of three rooms, or rather two, one being a common room, and the other being subdivided into two small, narrow chambers, lived Rose and Adeline Beaufort, respectively nineteen and seventeen years of age, and their young brother Harry, a boy of thirteen.

It is five o'clock in the afternoon when we look in upon them.

"Rose," said her sister, "you look very tired. Can't you leave off for an hour and rest?"

Rose was bending over a vest which she

was making. Her drooping figure and the lines on her face bespoke fatigue, yet her fingers swiftly plied the needle, and she seemed anxiously intent upon her task.

She shook her head in answer to her sister's words.

"No, Addie," she said; "it won't do for me to stop. You know how little I earn at the most. I can't make more than one vest in a day, and I get but thirty-five cents apiece."

"I know it, Rose," replied Adeline, with a sigh; "it is a great deal of work to do for that paltry sum. If I were able to help you we might get along better, even at such wages. I feel that I am very useless, and a burden on you and Harry."

"You mustn't think anything of the kind, Addie," said Rose, quickly, looking affectionately at her sister. "You know you are not strong enough to work."

"And so you have to work the harder, Rose"

"Never mind, Addie; I am strong, and I enjoy working for you."

"But still I am so useless."

"You chase us up, and we can work all the better."

"I earn nothing. I wonder if I shall always be so weak and useless?"

"No. Don't you remember the doctor said you would in all probability outgrow your weakness and be as strong as I am? All that is needed is patience."

"Ah, it is not so easy to be always patient —when I think, too, of how differently we should have been situated if grandfather had treated us justly."

A shadow came over the face of Rose.

"Yes; I don't like to think of that. Why should he have left all his property to our cousin Philip and none to us?"

"But if Philip should die it would all be ours, so Mr. Codicil says."

"I don't want anything to happen to the poor boy."

"Nor I, Rose. But don't you think he might do something for us?"

"So he would, very probably, if he were left to himself; but you know he is under the guardianship of that uncle of his, Richard Grafton, who is said to be intensely selfish and wholly unprincipled. He means to live as handsomely as he can at Philip's expense."

"Did grandfather appoint him guardian?"

"I believe so. Richard Grafton is very artful, and he led grandfather to believe him fitted to be an excellent guardian for the boy."

"I suppose he is in Europe?"

"No; I heard from Mr. Codicil, yesterday, that he was in New York."

"Is Philip with him?"

"Yes. He was to take the boy to Mr. Codicil's office to-day. There was a report some time since—I did not mention it to you for fear of exciting you—that Philip was dead. Mr. Codicil wrote to Mr. Grafton to make inquiry. In answer, he has come to New York, bringing Philip with him. While the boy lives, he receives an annual income of six thousand dollars for the boy's expenses, and to compensate him for his guardianship. You see, therefore, that Philip's death would make a great difference to him."

"And to us," sighed Adeline.

"Addie," said Rose, gravely, "don't allow yourself to wish for the death of our young cousin. It would be wicked."

"I know it, Rose; but when I consider how hard you work, and how confined Harry is as a cash-boy, I am strongly tempted."

"Then put away the temptation, and trust to a good Providence to take good care of us. God will not fail us."

"I wish I had your faith, Rose," said her younger sister.

"So you would, Addie, if you had my strength," said Rose, in an affectionate tone. "It is harder for you to be idle than for me to work."

"You are right there, Rose. I only wish I could work. Do you know where Philip and his guardian are staying?"

"Yes; Mr. Codicil told me they were staying at the Metropolitan Hotel."

"Did you ever see Philip?"

"Not since he was a little boy. I would not know him."

"Do you suppose he knows anything about us?"

"Probably Mr. Grafton never mentions us. Yet he must know that he has cousins living, but he may not know how hard we have to struggle for a livelihood."

"I wish we could get a chance to speak to him. He might feel disposed to help us."

"Probably his power is not great. He is only sixteen, and I presume has little command of money."

"How do you think it would do for Harry to carry him a letter, asking him to call upon us?"

"His guardian would intercept it."

"It might be delivered to him privately."

"There is something in what you say," returned Rose, thoughtfully. "He is our cousin, and we are his only living relatives. It would only be proper for him to call upon us."

"The sooner we communicate with him the better, then," said Adeline, whose temperament was quick and impulsive. "Suppose I write a letter and get Harry to carry it to the hotel when he comes home.".

"As you please, Addie. I would write it, but I want to finish this vest to-night."

"I will write it. I want to be of some little use."

She rose, and with languid step drew near the table. Procuring writing materials, she penned a brief note, which she handed to Rose, when completed, with the inquiry, "How will that do?"

Rose cast her eyes rapidly over the brief note, which read as follows:

"DEAR COUSIN PHILIP:—No doubt you are aware that you have three cousins in this city—my sister Rose, my brother Harry, who will hand you this note, and myself. We have not seen you for many years. Will it be too much to ask you to call on us? We are in humble quarters, but shall be glad to welcome you to our poor home.
"Your cousin,
"ADELINE BEAUFORT."

In a line below, the address was given.

"That will do very nicely, Addie," said Rose. "I am glad you did not hint at our need of assistance."

"If he comes to see us, he can see that for himself. I hope something may come of it," continued the younger sister.

" Don't count too much on it, or your disappointment will be the more keen."

" Harry can carry it around after supper."

" Philip may be at supper."

" Then he can wait. I wish he would come home."

As if in answer to her wish the door was hastily opened, and a bright, ruddy-faced boy entered.

" Welcome back, Harry," said Rose, with a smile. " How have you passed the day ?"

" Running round as usual, Rose. It's no joke to be a cash-boy."

" I wish I could run round, Harry," sighed Addie.

" So do I. That would be jolly. How are you feeling to-day, Addie ?"

" About the same. Are you very tired ?"

" Oh, no; only about the same as usual."

" Because I would like to have you do an errand for me."

" Of course I will," said Harry, cheerfully. " What is it ?"

" I want you to take this note to the Metropolitan Hotel."

7

"Who do you know there?" asked Harry, in surprise.

An explanation was given.

"I want you to be very particular to give the note to Philip without his guardian's knowledge. Can you manage it?"

"I'll try. I'll go the first thing after supper."

CHAPTER XII.

A SURPRISING ANNOUNCEMENT.

HARRY BEAUFORT entered the Metropolitan Hotel with the confidence of a city boy who knew that hotels are places of general resort, and that his entrance would not attract attention. He walked slowly through to the rear, looking about him guardedly to see if he could discover anybody who answered to his idea of Philip Grafton. Had he seen Ben, he would doubtless have supposed that he was the cousin of whom he was in search; but Ben had come in about five o'clock and had gone out again with his friend, the reporter, who had called for him.

Thus Harry looked in vain, and was disposed to think that he would have to leave the hotel with his errand unaccomplished. This he didn't like to do. He concluded, therefore, to go up to the desk and inquire of the clerk.

"Is there a boy staying here named Philip Grafton?" asked Harry.

"Yes, my boy. Do you want to see him?" returned the clerk.

"Yes, sir, if you please."

"He went out half an hour since," said a bell-boy, who chanced to be near.

"You can leave any message," said the clerk.

"I have a note for him," said Harry, in a doubtful tone.

"I will give it to him when he comes in."

Harry hesitated. He had been told to put the note into Philip's own hand. But there was no knowing when Philip would come in.

"I guess it'll do to leave it," he thought. "Please give it into his own hands," he said; and the clerk carelessly assented.

Harry left the hotel, and five minutes later Richard Grafton, or Major Richard Grafton, as he called himself, entered and walked up to the clerk's desk.

"Any letters or cards for me?" he asked.

"There's a note for your nephew," said the clerk, producing the one just left.

"Ha!" said the major, pricking up his ears suspiciously. "Very well, I will take it and give it to him."

Of course the clerk presumed that this was all right, and passed it over.

Major Grafton took the note carelessly and sauntered into the reading-room, where he deliberately opened it.

"I must see who is writing to Philip," he said to himself. "It may be necessary to suppress the note."

As he read the note, the contents of which are already familar to the reader, his brow darkened with anger and anxiety.

"It is fortunate that this came into my hands," he reflected. "It would have puzzled the boy, and had he gone to see these people the murder would have been out and probably my plans would have ended in disaster. There is something about the boy that leads me to doubt whether he would second my plans if he suspected what they were. I must devise some means for throwing these people off the scent and keeping the boy in the dark. What shall I do?"

After a little reflection, Major Grafton decided to remove at once to a different hotel. He resolved to do it that very night, lest there should be another attempt made to communicate with his young secretary. He must wait, however, till Ben returned.

Half an hour later Ben entered, and found the major walking impatiently up and down the office.

"I thought you would never come back," he said, impatiently.

"I am sorry if I inconvenienced you, sir," Ben said. "I didn't know you wished me back early."

"Come up stairs with me and pack. We are going to leave the hotel."

"Where are we going?" asked Ben in surprise.

"You will know very soon," answered the major.

Major Grafton notified the clerk that he wished a hack in fifteen minutes, as he was about to leave the hotel.

"Very well, major. Are you going to leave the city?"

" Not at once. I may spend a few days at the house of a friend," answered Grafton, evasively.

"Shall we forward any letters?"

" No; I will call here for them."

In fifteen minutes a porter called at the door of Major Grafton's room and took down the two trunks. A hack was in waiting.

" Where to, sir?" asked the driver.

" You may drive to the Windsor Hotel," was the answer.

The Windsor Hotel, on Fifth avenue, is over two miles farther up town than the Metropolitan. Leaning back in his comfortable seat, Ben enjoyed the ride, and was pleased with the quiet, aristocratic appearance of the Windsor. A good suite of rooms was secured, and he found himself even more luxuriously accommodated than at the Metropolitan.

" I wonder why we have changed our hotel," he thought.

As if aware what was passing through his mind, Major Grafton said:

" This hotel is much more conveniently located for my business than the other."

"It seems a very nice hotel," said Ben.

"There is none better in New York."

"I wonder what his business is," passed through Ben's mind, but he was afraid of offending by the inquiry.

Another thing puzzled him. He was ostensibly Major Grafton's private secretary, and as such was paid a liberal salary, but thus far he had not been called upon to render any service. There was nothing in this to complain of, to be sure. If Major Grafton chose to pay him for doing nothing, that was his lookout. Meanwhile he would be able to save up at least half of his salary, and transmit it to his mother.

When they were fairly installed in their new home Major Grafton said:

"I have a call to make, and shall be absent till late. I suppose you can take care of yourself?"

"Oh, yes, sir. If there is anything you wish me to do——"

"Not this evening. I have not got my affairs settled yet. That is all the better for you, as you can spend your time as you choose."

About an hour later, as Ben was in the billiard-room, looking with interest at a game, his cousin, Clarence Plantagenet, and Percy Van Dyke entered.

"How are you?" said Clarence, graciously. "Percy, this is my cousin, Ben Baker."

"Glad to see you, I'm sure," said Percy.

"Won't you join us in a little game?"

"No, thank you," answered Ben. "I don't play billiards."

"Then you ought to learn."

"I thought you said you were staying at the Metropolitan," said Plantagenet.

"So I was, but we have moved to the Windsor."

"Have you a good room?"

"Tip-top!"

"Does that mean on the top floor?" asked Percy, laughing.

"Not exactly. We are on the third floor."

"Come, Percy, here's a table. Let us have a game."

They began to play, and Ben sat down in a comfortable arm-chair and looked on. Though neither of the boys was an expect, they played a fair game, and Ben was interested in watching it.

"It's wonderful how he's improved," thought Clarence. "When I saw him in pa's office I thought he was awkward and gawky; now he looks just like one of us. He's had great luck in falling in with this Major Grafton. Really, I think we can afford to recognize him as a relation."

When the boys had played a couple of games, they prepared to go.

"By the way, Ben," said Clarence, "the governor told me to invite you to dinner on Sunday. Have you any other engagement?"

"Not that I know of. I will come if I can."

"That's right. Ta-ta, old fellow."

"He treats me a good deal better than he did when we first met," thought Ben. "There's a great deal of virtue in good clothes, I expect."

Ben was asleep before Major Grafton came home.

In the morning, when he awoke, he found that the major was already dressing.

"By the way, Philip," said his employer, quietly, "we sail for Europe this afternoon at three."

"Sail for Europe!" ejaculated Ben, overwhelmed with surprise.

"Yes. See that your trunk is packed by eleven."

CHAPTER XIII.

A FAREWELL CALL.

BEN was startled by Major Grafton's abrupt proposal. To go to Europe would be delightful, he admitted to himself, but to start at a few hours' notice was naturally exciting. What would his mother and sister say?

"I suppose there isn't time for me to go home and see my mother before sailing?" he ventured to say, interrogatively.

"As we are to sail at three o'clock this afternoon, you can judge for yourself about that," said the major, coolly. "Don't you want to go?"

"Oh, yes, sir. There is nothing I should like better. I should like to have said good-by to my mother, but——"

"Unfortunately, you can't. I am glad you take so sensible a view of the matter. I will depend on you to be ready."

"How long shall we probably be gone?" asked Ben.

"I can tell you better some weeks hence, Philip. By the way," he added, after a moment's thought, "if any letters should come here addressed to you, don't open them till I come back."

Ben looked at the major in surprise. Why should he not open any letters that came for him? He was not likely, he thought, to receive any except from Sunderland.

"I will explain," continued the major. "There are some people in the city that are continually writing begging letters to me. They use every method to annoy me, and might go so far as to write to you and ask your intercession."

"I understand," said Ben, unsuspiciously.

"I thought you would," returned the major, evidently relieved. "Of course if you get any letter from home you will open that."

"Thank you, sir."

After breakfast Major Grafton left the hotel without saying where he was going, and Ben addressed himself first to packing his trunk, and then going down to the reading-room. There he sat down and wrote a letter to his mother, which ran thus:

"DEAR MOTHER:—I can imagine how much you will be surprised when I tell you that when this letter reaches you I shall be on my way to Europe. Major Grafton, my employer, only told me an hour since, and we sail this afternoon at three. I should be glad to come home and bid you and my little sister good-by, but there is no time. I know you will miss me, but it is a splendid chance for me to go, and I shall be receiving a liberal salary, out of which I can send you money from time to time. I know I shall enjoy myself, for I have always had a longing to go to Europe, though I did not dream that I should have the chance so soon. I will write to you as soon as we get on the other side.

    "Your loving son,   BEN.
  "P. S.—We sail on the Parthia."

It may be readily understood that this letter made a great sensation in Sunderland. Mrs. Baker hardly knew whether to be glad or sorry. It was hard to part from Ben for an uncertain period. On the other hand, all her friends congratulated her on Ben's great success in securing so good a position and salary. It was certainly a remarkable stroke of good fortune.

Ben was about to write another letter to Clarence, explaining why he could not accept the invitation for dinner on Sunday, but a glance at the clock showed him that he would have a chance to go to his uncle's store, and that seemed, on the whole, more polite.

He jumped on board a Broadway car at Twenty-third street, and half an hour later got out in front of his uncle's large business establishment. He entered with quite a different feeling from that attending his first visit, when, in his country attire, poor and without prospects, he came to make an appeal to his rich uncle.

Handsome clothes are apt to secure outward respect, and one of the salesmen came forward, obsequiously, and asked:

"What can I show you, young gentleman?"

"Nothing, thank you," answered Ben, politely. "Is my uncle in?"

"Your uncle?"

"Mr. Walton."

"Oh, yes; you will find him in his office."

"Thank you."

Nicholas Walton looked up as Ben entered his presence, and did not immediately recognize the handsomely-dressed boy who stood before him. He concluded that it was one of Clarence's high-toned acquaintances.

"Did you wish to see Clarence?" he asked affably. "I am sorry to say that he has not been in this morning."

"I should like to see him, Uncle Nicholas; but I also wished to see you."

"Oh, it's Ben!" said Mr. Walton, in a slightly changed tone.

"Yes, uncle; I met my cousin at the Windsor last evening."

"He told me so. You are staying there, he says."

"For a very short time. My cousin was kind enough to invite me to dinner on Sunday."

"Yes; we shall be glad to have you dine with us."

"I am sorry I cannot come. I am to sail for Europe this afternoon."

"You sail for Europe!" repeated his uncle, in amazement.

"Yes, uncle. I knew nothing of it till this morning."

"It is indeed surprising. To what part do you go?"

"I believe we sail for Liverpool in the Parthia. More than that I know nothing."

"You are certainly strangely fortunate," said the merchant, musingly. "Does this Major Grafton appear to be wealthy?"

"I judge that he is."

"Does he pay you well?"

"He gives me fifty dollars per month."

"And what do you do?"

"I am his private secretary, but thus far I have not been called upon to do much. I suppose I shall have more to do when I get to Europe."

"He seems to be eccentric as well as rich. Perhaps he will want to adopt you. I advise you to try to please him."

"I shall certainly do that, though I don't think he will adopt me."

"Clarence will be sorry not to have seen

8

you. He has taken a trip to Long Branch this morning with Percy Van Dyke."

"I saw Percy last evening."

"This country nephew of mine gets into fashionable society remarkably quick," thought the merchant. "There must be something in the boy, or he would not make his way so readily."

"We are all going to Long Branch next week," said Mr. Walton, aloud. "We are to stay at the West End. If you had remained here you could have tried to persuade Major Grafton to spend part of the season at the Branch."

"I shall be satisfied with Europe," said Ben, smiling.

"You have reason to be satisfied. Clarence will envy you when he hears that you are going."

"It didn't look as if he were likely to envy me for anything when I met him here the other day," thought Ben.

"Please remember me to my cousin," said Ben, and shaking his uncle's extended hand he left the store.

He was passing through the store when he felt a touch on his shoulder.

Turning, he recognized the tall lady he had met just after his last visit.

" Are you not the boy who told me I had a ticket on my shawl?" she inquired.

"Yes, madam," replied Ben, smiling.

"I recognize your face, but otherwise you look very different."

"You mean I am better dressed."

" Yes; I thought you a country boy when I met you."

"So I am, but I am trying to be mistaken for a city boy."

"I am relieved to meet you, for some one told me you had got into some trouble with the unmannerly boys who were following me."

"I am much obliged to you for your solicitude in my behalf," said Ben, not caring to acknowledge the fact of the arrest.

"I had hoped to be of service to you, but I see you don't appear to need it. I am here buying a suit of clothes for a poor boy in whom I am interested. Let me give you my card, and if you ever need a friend, come and see me."

The card bore the name of "Jane Wilmot, 300 Madison avenue."

Ben thanked Miss Wilmot and left ˜his uncle's store.

CHAPTER XIV.

WHAT BEN'S FRIENDS THOUGHT.

"DID you see Philip?" asked Adeline, eagerly, when her young brother returned from his visit to the Metropolitan Hotel.

"No," answered Harry. "He was out."

"And you brought back the note, then?" said his sister, disappointed.

"No; the clerk said he would give it to him; so I left it with him."

Adeline looked anxious.

"I am afraid his guardian will get hold of it," she said, turning to Rose.

"Even if he does, there is nothing in it that you need regret writing."

"It would never reach Philip."

"Probably you are right. In that case we must make another effort when there seems a good chance."

It was decided that Harry should call the next day, at his dinner hour, and ascertain whether the note had been delivered. He did so, but only to learn that the note had been given to Major Grafton, and that both he and Philip had left the hotel.

"Do you know where they went," asked Harry, eagerly.

"No; the major did not say. He will probably send here for letters, and then I can mention that you called."

Harry assented, not being able to explain that this would not answer his purpose.

When he reported his information at home, Adeline said, quickly:

"He left because he does not want us to communicate with Philip."

"Probably," said Rose. "This shows," she added, "that he is afraid Philip would be inclined to do something for us. I am glad to have my faith strengthened in the boy, at all events. If he were willing to live in luxury while he knew we were struggling with poverty I could not regard him as a cousin."

The next morning Mr. Codicil read in the

morning papers, among the passengers who had sailed for Europe the day before, the names of Major Grafton and Philip.

"The fellow has lost no time," he said to himself. "The boy is bright and attractive, but he stands a chance of being spoiled under such a guardian. I wish I had questioned him, and tried to learn something of him. I might have given him some idea of the injustice which has been practiced toward his poor cousins. I do not care so much that he profits by it as that that worthless uncle of his should live in luxury at their expense. I am afraid they are having a hard time."

How hard a time the sisters were having— how stern and exacting was the toil which her sister's helplessness imposed upon Rose—Mr. Codicil really had little idea. If he had, he would certainly have done something to assist them, for he was a kind-hearted man; but whenever Rose called upon him she was neatly dressed, and did not bear outward marks of the poverty with which she had to contend.

So far as Nicholas Walton was concerned,

he was glad, upon the whole, to learn that his nephew had gone to Europe. He could not see Ben without his conscience reproaching him with the wrong he had done him, and was still doing him and his mother, by retaining possession of a sum of money which would have given them opulence in exchange for the poverty which was not removed by the small allowance he sent them.

"Perhaps Major Grafton will adopt the boy," he said to himself, "and then he won't need his father's money."

As if this would gloss over or excuse the base fraud of which he had been guilty. He had knowingly and intentionally been the occasion of his brother-in-law's sudden death, and was as much his murderer as if he had plunged a knife into his breast, though his crime was less brutal and revolting.

While these thoughts were passing through his mind, Clarence entered the office.

"Clarence, your cousin has been here to see you," said Mr. Walton.

"What did he have to say, pa?"

"He came to bid you good-by."

"To bid me good-by? What for? Where is he going?"

"He is to sail for Europe this afternoon."

"To sail for Europe!" repeated Clarence, in amazement. "He didn't say anything about it last evening."

"Because he did not know it. He was only told this morning."

"He's a lucky beggar!" said Clarence, enviously. "I've been longing to go to Europe this ever so long. Percy Van Dyke spent last summer in Switzerland. It annoys me to hear him talk of the splendid times he had. Here is my country cousin going, while I have to stay at home."

"Don't worry, Clarence," said his father, encouragingly. "You shall go in time. If your friend Percy should be going again, and will accept you as a companion, I will let you go."

This somewhat cheered up Clarence, though with the natural impatience of youth he wanted to go at once.

"I think I never knew a boy as lucky as Ben," said he.

"He certainly has been strangely fortunate," said Mr. Walton.

"He would have been glad to take a place in a store at five dollars a week, and now he's got something ever so much better. I believe he has more money than I to spend, and I am sure he dresses better."

"He seems to have made an impression upon this Major Grafton. I shouldn't be surprised if Grafton adopted him. He has no family of his own, and is, I imagine, very rich."

We know that on this last point Mr. Walton was misinformed. The suggestion, however, was enough to excite the envy and jealousy of Clarence.

"Do you think he will be richer than I?" he asked.

"You will be well provided for, Clarence. You won't have occasion for envying your cousin, even if he should be adopted by Major Grafton."

We have now to change the scene to the little town of Sunderland, from which our hero had come to New York to seek the good fortune which he so strangely found.

We direct our steps to a plain cottage, containing but four rooms and an attic, which stood a little out of the centre of the village. Small and plain as it was, it had an air of refinement and good taste, with its climbing honeysuckles, tiny bed of flowers, its trimly-kept lawn and neat surroundings, which are vainly sought about many more pretentious residences.

Here dwelt Mrs. Baker and Ben's little sister, Alice, but ten years old. She bore a strong family resemblance to Ben, and was equally good-looking.

"It seems an age since Ben left home," said Mrs. Baker, with a little sigh.

"I miss him dreadfully, mother," said Alice. "Why need he go away?"

"I can't blame him, Alice, though I am very sorry to have him go," said Mrs. Baker. "He is ambitious——"

"What does that mean?" asked Alice, puzzled.

"It means that he is anxious to get on in the world—to make money. It is a natural feeling for a boy."

"He used to earn money here at home," said Alice.

"Only a little.   No doubt he can do better in New York, if he can get a chance.   If his uncle will only help him——"

"I should think he might, mother. Ben is a good boy."

"There is none better," assented his mother, fondly ; "but strangers may not know that."

Just then a neighbor, driving by, paused in the road and called out to the widow, whom he saw at the open window :

"Widder Baker, there's a letter for you at the post-office.   'Spect it's from Ben."

"Go right over and get it, Alice," said her mother, excitedly.

Alice wasn't long in performing her errand. She came back well rewarded, bringing with her two letters, one of which had arrived the day before.   The first letter contained an account of his cold reception by his uncle, and on the other hand his good luck in encountering Major Grafton.   As an earnest of his good fortune he enclosed three five-dollar bills.

"God has been very good to us !" said the

widow, with beaming face. "I can hardly believe in Ben's good fortune."

"Open the other letter, mother," said Alice.

Mrs. Baker did so, and, glancing over it rapidly, uttered a quiet exclamation of surprise and dismay.

"Alice," she said, "Ben has sailed for Europe !"

"Gone to Europe, and without bidding us good-by !"

"He did not have any chance," and Mrs. Baker read Ben's letter.

When she came to think it over, she felt that Ben was, on the whole, fortunate to have so good an opportunity of seeing the world; and as to dangers and risks, God would take care of him abroad as well as at home. She would have liked to have known the man who had her boy in charge. Doubtless he must have taken a fancy to Ben, or he would not have given him such a chance.

CHAPTER XV.

FILIPPO NOVARRO.

NICHOLAS WALTON was well pleased with the good fortune of his nephew. Though a selfish man, he was not wholly without a conscience and a heart. He had always regretted the manner in which he had possessed himself of the large sum of money which, by enabling him to take a store on Broadway, and largely extend his business, had allowed him to take a place among the foremost merchants of New York. He would have preferred to compass his own fortune without bringing ill-fortune to his brother-in-law, but if the thing had to be done again, under the same circumstances, he would probably have yielded to the same temptation.

"Ben appears to be a smart, attractive boy," said Walton to himself. "He is likely to make his own way in the world, especially

in his present position. I dare say it is better for him to have lived plainly, and nour-
ished self-reliance, than to have been reared
in luxury. Then, as to the fortune, Doctor
Baker was a man of very little business
shrewdness. He would have wasted the money
in bad investments, and, ten to one, not a dollar of it would have remained at the present
time."

All this Nicholas Walton said to quiet his
conscience, but without success. Many a time,
especially in the silent watches of the night,
memory revived for him that scene, which he
would so gladly have forgotten, when his ill-
fated brother-in-law died in a fit of agitation
brought on by Walton intentionally. He could
see himself once more rifling the pockets of the
dead man, and converting to his own use the
money which would have made the physician
and his family prosperous and happy.

These disquieting thoughts he tried to get
rid of. He tried to persuade himself that he
was wholly disinterested in his good wishes
for his nephew. By way of keeping up the
illusion he snatched five minutes from his

business, and wrote the following letter of congratulation to his sister:

"MY DEAR SISTER:—Benjamin has no doubt apprised you of his success in obtaining a profitable engagement, and of his departure for Europe. He has also, perhaps, told you that I was opposed to his remaining in the city. I admit that I thought it would have been better for him to remain in Sunderland and obtain a practical acquaintance with farming, in which case I would, at the proper time, have set him up on a farm of his own, for I hold that the farmer is the only truly independent man. A merchant may be rich to-day and a bankrupt to-morrow, and that in spite of the utmost care and prudence. However, I won't dwell on this subject. I am willing to admit that I did not give my nephew credit for the energy and ability he has shown. Though I refused to help him, further than to pay the expenses of his trip to the city, on condition of his returning home at once, he remained and succeeded in commending himself to the favor of a rich man who has given him an excellent position, and will probably—for he seems to be eccentric—finally conclude to adopt the boy.

"It is needless to say that I could not have anticipated such extraordinary luck for Benjamin, and that I am glad he followed his own counsel and remained in the city. Doubtless a better fortune awaits him than the life of a farmer, which, though independent, is laborious. I only write now to congratulate you upon his success, and to express my interest in him. Though you will no doubt miss him, I think you will be able to see that he has done the best thing for himself and for you in the engagement which he has made with Major Grafton. He would have dined at my house to-morrow, but for his sudden departure.

"I inclose my next month's allowance a little in advance.

"Your affectionate brother,

"NICHOLAS WALTON."

Mrs. Baker was surprised and gratified on receiving this unusually long letter from her brother Nicholas. She had been wounded at the cool reception which he had accorded to Ben, as detailed in the letter of the latter, but this letter put a new face on the matter.

"After all, Nicholas feels an interest in Ben," she said to herself, "and no doubt he acted for what he thought the best in the advice he gave him to remain in Sunderland and become a farmer. He acknowledges his mistake very handsomely."

So upon the spur of the moment she wrote her brother a letter, acknowledging gratefully

9

his kindness to her boy, and asking for a continuance of it.

This letter was received by Mr. Walton with satisfaction. It made it easier for him to feel that he had not, after all, wronged his sister and her family as much as his conscience sometimes reproached him with.

"Would that I could lose all the memories of that dreadful hour!" he said to himself, with a shudder.

But he did not find that so very easy. It was destined to be recalled to him in a startling manner within a week.

As he sat in his office the following Thursday, a clerk entered.

"Mr. Walton," he said, "there is a foreign gentleman in the store who wishes to see you."

"Is it a stranger?"

"Yes, sir."

"He wishes to see me on business, doubtless. You may bring him in."

The visitor entered—a man of medium size and swarthy complexion—who would be taken at first sight for a Spaniard or a Portuguese.

Nicholas Walton regarded him with a look of inquiry.

"Do I speak to Mr. Walton?" asked the stranger, in good English, but with a foreign accent.

"I am Mr. Walton," answered the merchant.

"You are brother-in-law to Mr.—I beg pardon, Doctor Baker?"

"Ye-es," answered the merchant, with a startled look.

"Can you tell me if the good doctor is well?"

"He is—dead!" replied Walton, slowly. "Did you know him?"

"I much regret to hear of his death. I did not know him, but I met him once."

"This must be the man who gave him the bonds," thought Walton, trying to conceal his perturbation. "The moment and the man I have so long dreaded have arrived. Now, Nicholas Walton, you require all your coolness and nerve."

"May I ask when that was?" he asked, with apparent unconcern.

"Five years ago. I was the agent for conveying to him a large sum in securities bequeathed him by my uncle, to whom he had rendered a great service."

"Indeed! I am most glad to see you, sir. I wish my brother-in-law were alive to give you personal welcome."

"When—did he die?"

"But a short time after you met him. He died instantly—of heart disease."

"He left a wife and child, did he not?"

"He left a wife and two children."

"And they live?"

"Yes."

"I wish I could see them."

Nicholas Walton was perplexed and alarmed. If the stranger should see Mrs. Baker, his elaborate scheme would fall to the ground and he would be called upon for an explanation.

"Do you remain long in the city?" he asked.

"I go to Havana in three days. Business of importance, not to mention the sickness of my brother, calls me there."

"Ah!" said the merchant, relieved. "You will have to defer seeing Mrs. Baker, then."

"I thought she might live near by," said Filippo Novarro, for such was the name he gave.

"Two years ago she removed to Minnesota," said the merchant, with fluent falsehood. "Her son, however, is travelling in Europe."

"That, at least, will look as if she retained her fortune," he said to himself.

"Then I must not hope to meet her," said Novarro. "When you write, will you give her my profound respects?"

"With pleasure, Señor Novarro," said Walton, briskly. "Can I be of any service to you personally?"

"Thank you, sir, no. I shall be very busy till I leave the city."

"Then let me express my pleasure in meeting you," said Walton, offering his hand.

"The pleasure is mutual, Mr. Walton, I assure you," said the stranger, bowing low.

"Thank Heaven, I have got rid of you," said Walton to himself, wiping the perspiration from his brow. "But shall I always be as lucky?"

CHAPTER XVI.

ON BOARD THE PARTHIA.

"AM I really on the Atlantic, bound for Europe?" said Ben to himself, as he paced the deck of the Parthia, then several hours out.

He found it hard to realize, for only a week before he had been in his quiet country home, wholly unconscious of the great change that fate had in store for him.

He was not unfavorably affected by the new sea-life. Instead of making him sick, it only gave him a pleasant sense of exhilaration. With Major Grafton it was different. He was a very poor sailor. He was scarcely out of port before he began to feel dizzy, and was obliged to retire to his state-room. He felt almost irritated when he saw how much better Ben bore the voyage than he.

"One would think you were an old sailor,

instead of me," he said. " I have crossed the Atlantic a dozen times, and yet the first whiff of sea air lays me on my back, while you seem to enjoy it."

"So I do at present," answered Ben ; " but perhaps my time will come to be sick. Can't I do something to make you comfortable ?"

"You may tell the steward to bring some ginger ale," said the major.

Ben promptly complied with the major's request. He felt glad to do something to earn the liberal salary which he was receiving. It was not exactly acting as a private secretary ; but, at any rate, he was able to be of service, and this pleased him. He had no complaint to make of Major Grafton. The latter saw that he wanted for nothing, and had he been the major's son he would have fared no better. Yet he did not form any attachment for his employer, as might have been thought natural. He blamed himself for this, when he considered the advantages of his position ; but it was not so strange or culpable as Ben supposed. The boy saw clearly that, whatever might have been Major Grafton's motives in

taking him into his service, it was not any
special interest or attachment. The reader
understands that Grafton had a purpose to
serve, and that a selfish one. For Ben he
cared nothing, but his own interest required
that he should have a boy with him as a substitute for the one whose death he wished to
conceal, and our hero filled the bill as well as
any he could secure.

One day, while Major Grafton was in his
state-room, enduring as well as he could the
pangs of sea-sickness, a gentleman on deck
accosted Ben:

"You seem to enjoy the voyage, young
man," he said.

"Yes, sir; very much."

"You are not alone?"

"No; I am travelling with Major Grafton."

"Indeed!" said the gentleman, in surprise.
"I didn't know the major was on board.
Where does he keep himself?"

"He seldom leaves his state-room. He has
been sick ever since he started."

"I remember meeting the major last summer in Switzerland. You were sick at the time, but from your present appearance I judge that you got bravely over it."

"I think you are mistaken, sir. I was not with Major Grafton at that time."

"You were not! That is strange. Surely there was a boy with him; I remember he called him Philip."

"He calls me so, but that is not my name."

"Do you mean to say that you were not with the major at that time?"

"I did not know there was such a man at that time."

"Humph! I don't understand it," said James Bolton (this was the traveller's name). "I do remember, however, hearing that the boy, then called Philip, died at Florence."

"I think that settles it," said Ben. "Whoever the poor fellow may have been that died, I am sure that it was not I."

"Are you Major Grafton's adopted son, or ward?"

"No, sir; I am his private secretary. That is, I was hired in that capacity, though as yet I have not had much writing to do."

"You are lucky. Take care you don't die, like the other boy."

"I will try to live, I assure you, sir."

"By the way, just mention my name to the major—James Bolton, of London. I dare say he will remember me. Just say that I occupied the room opposite his in the Hotel des Bergues, in Geneva, and that we went to Chamounix together. I should be glad to renew my acquaintance with him, whenever he feels well enough to come on deck."

"I will mention you to him, Mr. Bolton," said Ben, politely.

Our young hero took an early opportunity of keeping his promise.

On his next visit to the state-room he said:

"Major Grafton, I met a gentleman on deck this morning who wishes to be remembered to you."

"Who is it?" asked the major, quickly, raising his head from the pillow of his berth.

"He says his name is Bolton—James Bolton, of London."

"Don't know him!" said the major, shortly.

"He says that he was with you at the Hotel

des Bergues, in Geneva, Switzerland, last summer; also that he went with you to Chamounix."

"What else did he say?" asked the major, who seemed unpleasantly affected by the mention of Bolton's name.

"He thought I was with you at the time."

"Ha! What did you say?"

"I told him he was mistaken."

"Don't tell these fellows too much; they are simply impertinent," said the major, with a frown. "What more did he say?"

"He said you had a boy with you whom you called Philip, and that this boy, as he afterward heard, died at Florence."

Ben looked inquiringly at the major, as if to obtain confirmation or denial of this story.

Major Grafton hesitated, as if not decided what to say.

"It is true," he said, after a pause. "Poor Philip died; but it is a painful subject. I don't like to speak of it. You resemble him very closely, and that was my chief object in taking you as a companion. I don't really

need a private secretary, as you have probably found out."

"I wish you did, sir. I would like to do
something to earn my wages."

"Don't trouble yourself on that score. It
suits me to have a companion; I hate being
alone. As long as you conform to my wishes,
I will provide for you."

"Thank you, sir."

"But hark you, Philip! I don't care to
have you talk too much to strangers about me
or my affairs. Now, as to this man Bolton, I
prefer that you should keep him at a distance.
He is not a fit companion for you."

"Is he a bad man?" asked Ben, in some
surprise, for Bolton had seemed to him a very
respectable sort of man.

"He is a thoroughly unprincipled man,"
answered the major, emphatically. "He is a
confirmed gambler, and is cultivating your
society because he thinks you may have
money. He is trying to lead you into a
snare."

"Then I was deceived in him," said Ben,
indignantly, for it didn't occur to him to

doubt the positive statement of Major Grafton.

"Quite natural, Philip," said Grafton, pleased with having aroused the boy's suspicions of a man who might impart dangerous information. "Of course, I needn't suggest to you to keep the man at a distance. I do not care to have you come under his influence."

"I shall bear in mind what you say, sir," said Ben.

"I think I have checkmated this meddling Bolton," said the major to himself, in a tone of satisfaction.

When, a few hours later, Bolton approached Ben and asked: "Have you spoken to Major Grafton about me?" Ben coldly answered, "Yes, sir."

"Did he remember me?" questioned Bolton.

"Yes, sir."

"I thought he would. Are we likely to see him on deck soon?"

"No, sir, I think not."

Ben spoke so coldly that Bolton regarded

him with a puzzled look.   He could not help
seeing that the boy did not care to continue
the conversation, and, with a bow of farewell,
joined another passenger in a promenade.

"I should like to have asked him a little
more about the boy I am succeeding," thought
Ben; but he respected the major's wishes, and
kept aloof from Bolton for the remainder of
the voyage.

CHAPTER XVII.

THE BEAUFORTS IN TROUBLE.

THERE was an anxious look on Rose Beaufort's pleasant face. She and her young brother were the only bread-winners in the family, and work as hard as they might it was very difficult to make both ends meet. But for one item they could have managed with strict economy, but that item—the rent—was a formidable one. They hired their humble apartment of a Mrs. Flanagan, who leased the whole floor, and agreed to pay two dollars a week. This woman was a coarse, selfish person, whose heart was as hard and unfeeling as her face and manners were unprepossessing.

One Monday morning, about two months after Ben's departure for Europe, the landlady knocked at the door of the two sisters.

"It's Mrs. Flanagan," said Rose, with a troubled look, recognizing her knock. "She has come for her rent, and I have but fifty cents toward it."

"Perhaps she will wait," suggested Adeline; but her voice was not hopeful.

"Come in!" said Rose.

"You were mighty long tellin' me to come in," grumbled the landlady, as she entered the humble room, with a hostile look.

"I am sorry if I kept you waiting," said Rose, gently.

"I thought maybe you didn't want to see me," said Mrs. Flanagan. "I won't stay long to trouble ye."

"Stay as long as you like," said Rose in a conciliatory manner.

"I didn't come for any palaver—I haven't the time. I suppose you know what I came for. You haven't forgot it's Monday mornin'?" said the landlady, in an aggressive tone.

"I didn't forget it, Mrs. Flanagan, but I am afraid I shall have to disappoint you this morning."

"Do you mane to say you haven't got my rint ready?" demanded Mrs. Flanagan, her red face becoming still more inflamed with anger.

"Indeed, Mrs. Flanagan, it isn't my fault," pleaded Rose. "I've got fifty cents toward it, and if——"

"Fifty cints! What's fifty cints?" exclaimed the landlady, angrily. "Can I pay my rint wid fifty cints? It's a shame—that it is—for you to chate a poor hard-workin' woman, and a widder besides."

"My sister never cheats anybody," said Adeline, indignantly.

"Hoity-toity! So it's you that are spakin', is it?" said Mrs. Flanagan, with her arms akimbo. "You can talk, anyway, if you can't work. All you do is to sit here all day long, while your sister is wearin' out her fingers wid the needle."

It was a cruel blow to the poor girl, who needed no reminder of what she often thought about with bitter regret and mortification. She did not retort angrily, but, turning sadly to her sister, said:

"I am afraid it's true, Rose; I am only a burden and an expense to you. I do nothing to help you."

Now it was Rose's turn to be angry.

"Are you not ashamed, Mrs. Flanagan, to twit my poor sister with what is her misfortune, not her fault?" she exclaimed, with, flushed face and sparkling eyes. "She would gladly work, if she could."

"It's ashamed I'm to be, am I?" retorted Mrs. Flanagan, viciously. "I pay my bills, anyhow, and it's ashamed I'd be if I didn't. I don't want no more talk from the like of you. It's money I want."

"Here are fifty cents, and I will try to get you the rest to-day," said Rose, sadly.

"Them that wear gold rings can pay their rint, if they want to," was Mrs. Flanagan's parting shot, as she slammed the door behind her.

Rose looked at the plain gold ring on her finger. It had been her mother's ring, and for that she valued it above its intrinsic value.

"I can't part with this," she murmured, with moistened eyes. "Yet, is it right to keep it when we owe money?"

"Don't part with mother's ring, whatever you do, Rose," said her sister, hastily.

"But have we a right to keep it?" asked Rose, doubtfully.

"Yes, a thousand times, yes! That woman can wait for her money. We cannot part with this legacy of our dying mother."

"But she may put us out into the street," said Rose, shuddering.

"Is there nothing else by which we can raise money?" said Adeline, realizing their situation.

"Money is due me for two vests. As a general thing, Walton & Co. don't pay me till I hand in half a dozen, but perhaps they would make an exception in this case."

"That would be but seventy cents. It would not make up what we owe Mrs. Flanagan."

"It might induce her to wait for the rest," said Rose. "If you don't mind staying alone a little while, Addie, I will wrap them up and carry them to the store."

"Go, if you like, Rose. I always miss you, but I cannot expect to keep you here with me all the time."

Rose wrapped up the two completed vests, and putting on her hat, kissed her sister and went down stairs.

It was not far to the great store, which we have already entered with Ben.

Entering, Rose walked to the back part of the store and took the elevator to the second floor, where she found the superintendent of the work-room.

She made known her request.

"Quite out of the question, miss," said the superintendent, sharply.

He was a hard-featured man, who was a good man of business, but was not open to sentimental consideration.

"Didn't you know our rules?" he asked.

"Yes, sir; but this was a case of necessity."

"I beg your pardon, miss, it is a matter of business. When you have finished the batch we will pay you, and not till then."

"But, sir, I need the money very much."

"That is your affair, not ours. Probably you have friends and can borrow money, if you need it sooner than we are ready to pay it to you."

"I don't know where to find them," thought Rose, but she did not say this.

The superintendent had already turned away, as if to intimate that he had no more time to give her. Rose walked to the elevator slowly and sadly, and descended to the main store.

"What shall I do?" she thought. "Mrs. Flanagan will turn us out, and then poor Addie will suffer."

As she stepped out into the street the thought of the ring came back to her. It was dear to her as a cherished legacy from a mother early lost and deeply mourned, yet it had a money value which would relieve their pressing necessities for a week at least.

"I don't think mother would wish me to keep it under the circumstances," she thought. "Addie will scold me, but it appears to be the only thing that remains for me to do. Heaven knows that I don't wish to part with it."

The proper place to go would have been to a pawnbroker's shop, but Rose did not know of one. She had never had dealings with any. As she passed a jewelry store it occurred to her that perhaps they would buy it inside, and she entered.

"In what way can I serve you, miss?" asked a young man behind the counter.

"I—I wish to dispose of a ring," said Rose, hurriedly. "Can you tell me the value of it?" and she slipped the ring from her finger and offered it to the salesman.

"We don't buy second-hand jewelry," said the clerk, rudely. "We sell rings here; don't buy them."

"Then would you be kind enough to lend me two dollars on it till—till next week?" entreated Rose. "It must be worth much more than that."

"It doesn't matter how much it is worth," said the clerk. "We ain't in that line of business. You don't suppose we keep a pawnbroker's shop, do you?" and he laughed contemptuously, glancing at a tall lady who stood beside Rose and had listened attentively to the conversation, as if inviting her to enjoy the joke with him.

"Then perhaps you will direct me to a pawnbroker's," said Rose, ill at ease.

"Oh, you can go find one on the Bowery," said the clerk, carelessly. "Now, madam," turning to the tall lady, "what can I show you?"

His tone was much more respectful than the one he employed in speaking to Rose, for the lady, though far from beautiful, and no longer young, was handsomely dressed, and had the appearance of being wealthy.

"You can't show me anything to-day, young man," said Miss Jane Wilmot, for it was she. "I wish to speak to this young lady. My dear, come out of the store with me. I wish to ask you a few questions."

The clerk arched his brows in surprise and disappointment as his hoped-for customer walked away without purchasing anything, followed by Rose.

CHAPTER XVIII.

MRS. FLANAGAN IS DRIVEN FROM THE FIELD.

MISS JANE WILMOT had never been pretty, even when, twenty years before, she could lay claim to being a young lady; and her manners were decided; but a kind smile lighted up her face as she said to Rose:

"My child, you seem to be in trouble."

"Yes, indeed, madam," said Rose, "I am in great trouble."

"Don't think me inquisitive," said Miss Wilmot, "if I inquire into your trouble. I infer that you are in need of money."

"Yes, madam, I am very much in need of money, or I would not think of selling my mother's ring."

"Your mother—is she living?"

"No; she has been dead for five years."

"You are not alone in the world?"

"No, thank Heaven! I don't know how I

could bear to feel myself alone. I have a sick sister and a little brother."

"And does the whole burden of their support fall on you?" asked Miss Wilmot, in a tone of sympathy.

"Not quite. My little brother Harry earns two dollars a week as a cash-boy."

"That is not much help."

"It is nearly as much as I earn myself. There is not much to be earned at making vests at thirty-five cents each."

"Thirty-five!" repeated Miss Wilmot, indignantly. "Who pays you such a wretched price?"

"Walton & Co."

"No wonder they prosper, if they pay so little for having their work done. How many vests can you make in a week?"

"One vest a day is about as much as I can make, but I have made seven in a week."

"And you consider that a good week's work?" asked Miss Wilmot.

"Yes, but I cannot average that."

"That makes—let me see—two dollars and forty-five cents. You don't mean to say, child,

that your united incomes amount to only four
dollars and forty-five cents?"

"It generally amounts to less, for I cannot
average seven vests a week."

"Well, well, what are we coming to?" ejaculated Miss Wilmot, pityingly. "You don't
look, child, as if you had always been so mis-
erably poor."

"I have not. My grandfather was rich, but
he took offense at mother's marriage to father
and he left all his property to my cousin."

"The old wretch! Excuse me, child, I forgot that he was your grandfather. So you
were wholly left out of the will?"

"If my cousin should die, the whole property would come to us."

"He should have left the property between
you. But I fancy you think I am a curious
old woman, with my questions."

"I don't think you an old woman at all,
madam."

Miss Wilmot smiled. Though she was a
spinster of over forty she was not wholly without appreciation of a compliment, and the reply of Rose pleased her.

"At any rate, I am old enough to be your mother, my dear," she said. "But that is neither here nor there. How much did you expect to get for that ring?"

"I hoped that I might get three dollars," said Rose, hesitatingly. "I owe Mrs. Flanagan—she is my landlady—a dollar and a half, and I could pay that and have a little fund left to fall back upon."

"A little fund—a dollar and a half!" said Miss Wilmot, pityingly.

"I suppose I would not get so much at a pawnbroker's?" continued Rose.

"My child, I am not a pawnbroker, but I think it will be better for me to lend you something on the ring."

"If you only would, madam! I feel timid about going to a pawnshop."

"Where they would offer some ridiculous trifle for it, no doubt. Here, child, give me the ring."

Rose drew it from her finger and handed it to Miss Wilmot.

The latter drew a purse from her pocket and slipped the ring into it.

"It is too small for me to wear," she said. "It will be safe in my purse."

She drew out two five-dollar bills and handed them to Rose.

"Ten dollars!" exclaimed Rose, in surprise.

"I don't do business on the regular terms," said Miss Wilmot, smiling. "I am sure the ring is worth more than ten dollars to you. Some day you may be able to redeem it."

"I am afraid not, madam; but this money seems like a small fortune to me."

"You don't know what future luck is in store for you. I will keep the ring for you. You should know who has it. I am Miss Jane Wilmot, of 300 Madison avenue. I am called a strong-minded woman; I hope that won't prejudice you against me."

"It would be hard for me to become prejudiced against you after your liberality, Miss Wilmot. I wish there were more strong-minded woman like you."

"Now for your name, my child."

"I am Rose Beaufort; my sister's name is Adeline, and my little brother, twelve years old, is Harry."

"I have a great mind to go home with you, if you won't consider it an intrusion," said Miss Wilmot.

"Far from it, Miss Wilmot—that is, if you won't mind our humble quarters."

"If you can endure them week after week, I can get along for half an hour," said the spinster. "Lead the way, my dear. Is it far? If so, we will take a horse-car."

"It is less than half a mile, I should think," said Rose.

"Then we will walk."

They soon reached the poor tenement-house.

"You see it is a poor place," said Rose, apologetically.

"Poor enough!" said Miss Wilmot, plainly.

"You may not care to come up."

"There is nothing delicate about me, my child. Go on, I will follow."

Rose entered the poor room in advance of her visitor.

"Home again, Rose?" said Adeline, whose head was turned away from the door, and who therefore did not see Miss Wilmot.

"Yes, Addie."

"Did you get any money? Did they pay you for the vests?"

"No; but I met a good friend, who has come home with me. Miss Wilmot, this is my sister, Addie."

"I am glad to make your acquaintance, my dear," said the spinster, and her face, plain as it was, looked positively attractive from very kindness.

"You look good!" said Addie, whose instincts were rapid. "I am sure you are a friend."

"I will be," said Miss Wilmot, emphatically.

The weakness of the younger sister appealed to her even more strongly than the beauty of the elder.

Just then a knock was heard at the door. Mrs. Flanagan had heard the step of Rose upon the stairs, and had come up to see if she had brought money for the rent.

"It is my landlady, Mrs. Flanagan," said Rose.

"I want to see what sort of a woman she is.

Ask for delay, and let me go into this inner room," said Miss Wilmot, rapidly.

When Mrs. Flanagan entered the room there was no sign of a visitor.

"Well," said the landlady, entering upon her business at once, "have you got my money for me?"

But for Miss Wilmot's admonition, Rose would have produced the money without delay, but she thought it necessary to follow the directions of her new friend.

"They would not pay me for the two vests I had made," she said. "I must wait till all are finished."

"Just what I expected," said the landlady, placing her arms akimbo. "I saw how it would turn out. You needn't think I am going to be put off like this. Pay me my rent, or out you go, bag and baggage!"

"Would you turn my poor sister into the street, Mrs. Flanagan?"

"I am not going to keep you here for nothing, you may rely upon that."

"Won't you wait till next week?"

"When another week's rent will be due?

No, I won't, and I hope that you understand it."

"Then you ought to be ashamed of yourself, woman!" said a strong, decided voice, and Miss Wilmot strode out of the bedroom.

Mrs. Flanagan stared at her with mingled surprise and indignation.

"I am no more a woman than you are," she retorted.

"That's true enough," rejoined Miss Wilmot, "nor half as much. There's nothing womanly about you."

"Do you think I can let my rooms for nothing?" said the landlady, sullenly. She saw that Miss Wilmot was richly dressed, and she had a respect for such evidence of wealth.

"How much do the young ladies owe you?"

"A dollar and a half."

"What is the rent of these rooms?"

"Two dollars a week."

"Then, three dollars and a half will pay to the end of the present week?"

"Yes, ma'am."

"Here is the money. They will move out at the end of the week."

"I shall be glad to have them stay," said the landlady, now anxious to retain them.

"I shall find them a better home. Good-morning."

Mrs. Flanagan went down stairs feeling that she was worsted in the contest. She was a bold woman, but she was rather afraid of Miss Wilmot.

"Now, my dears," said the spinster, "let us talk business."

CHAPTER XIX.

BRIGHTER PROSPECTS.

"YOU must know, my dear," said Miss Wilmot, "that I am a rich woman, and own considerable more than my share of worldly goods. Among other items of property, I own a French flat house on West Twenty-fifth street. It isn't one of the costly flats, but is intended for people with moderate incomes. I learned yesterday that one of the flats was just vacated. The family occupying it is about to move to the West, and desired me, as a matter of convenience to them, to purchase their furniture, and let it furnished. I intended to decline, but now I shall accept, having found a tenant that suits me."

"Who is it?" asked Rose, not quite understanding her own connection with the matter.

"Her name is Rose Beaufort," said Miss Wilmot, smiling.

" But, Miss Wilmot, I am afraid it will be beyond my means. What rent shall you ask ?"

" I don't think thirty dollars a month will be too much, considering that there are five well-furnished rooms. There is even a piano."

" Thirty dollars a month !" exclaimed Rose, in dismay. "Why, that will be more than all of us together can earn. Mrs. Flanagan only asks us two dollars a week, and that we've hardly been able to meet."

" I think that can be made easy for you," said the spinster. " I shall let you pay in work."

" But I couldn't do enough to pay the rent alone."

" Not at making vests at thirty-five cents apiece, I admit. My work will be better paid for. I shall want some writing done, account-books straightened, and—by the way, do you play on the piano ?"

" Oh, yes, madam."

" Well ?"

" I believe I have a taste for it."

" Do you consider yourself competent to teach the piano ?"

"Yes, I think so."

"Why, then, did you not seek pupils, instead of trying to make a living by sewing?"

"So I did, but I had no one to recommend me, and I could not afford to advertise."

"Do you also play, my dear?" asked Miss Wilmot, turning to Adeline.

"But very little," answered the young girl, humbly.

"Addie draws and paints," said Rose. "I have no talent for either."

"Why, that is well. I may be able to obtain pupils for her, too. However, we can wait and see."

"Miss Wilmot," said Rose, gratefully, "you came to us like a good angel. I was almost despairing when I met you. Now, I am full of courage."

"Never despair!" said Miss Wilmot, kindly. "The sun is often behind the clouds. But I must be going. You will hear from me in a day or two."

The good spinster rose as she spoke, and going out of the humble room, descended the dirty staircase, leaving behind her joy where she had found sorrow.

"It seems almost too good to be true, Rose," said Addie.

"So it does, Addie."

"A nice furnished flat and a piano! I shall not believe it until I see it."

"We can rely upon whatever Miss Wilmot promises. Has she not paid our rent, and given us ten dollars besides?"

"How glad Harry will be when he hears it!"

"Yes, poor boy. It hasn't been a very pleasant home for him. Do you know, Addie, I feel inclined to be extravagant?"

"In what way, Rose?"

"I am going to order a nice dinner from a restaurant—roast turkey and vegetables; and I will make some coffee, and we will have everything ready by the time Harry arrives."

"But it will cost a great deal, Rose," said Adeline, in alarm.

"Never mind, for once. This ought to be a Thanksgiving Day for us. Let us celebrate it as such. Besides," added Rose, the frugal instinct coming in, "if I order two plates it will be enough for three of us. I know of a restaurant where we can get all I want for, say, seventy-five cents. We won't mind about money to-night."

"It will seem good to have a nice dinner once more," said Adeline, thoughtfully. "It is a long time since we had anything but the plainest food."

Rose postponed her feast until six o'clock, the hour when Harry usually got home. There was a restaurant near by, where she gave the order, directing it to be sent in at ten minutes to six.

Mrs. Flanagan was considerably surprised when a colored waiter made his appearance at her door with a large covered dish.

"Who is this for? Haven't you made a mistake?" she asked.

"No, ma'am. It's for a young lady—Miss Beaufort. Doesn't she live here?"

"Yes. What have you got there?" asked the landlady, curiously.

"Roast turkey."

"Bless my soul!" thought Mrs. Flanagan.

"She must have come into a fortune. It's all right!" and she directed the waiter to the room of the Beauforts.

When Harry arrived the little table was set out with its usual neatness, and on it there was a display such as made him start back with surprise.

"Where did all this come from?" he asked, bewildered.

"Explanations postponed till after supper," said Rose. "Sit down and we will begin."

"All right; I've no objection," said Harry. "Yes, Rose, you may give me some of the dressing. I say, ain't it good, though? I wish we could live like this every day."

A great fuss to make over a very ordinary dinner, some of my young readers may think; but let them put themselves in the place of this family, and judge whether they would not hail with joy such a meal after a long course of the most frugal fare.

They were in the midst of their enjoyment when a knock was heard at the door—a subdued knock; not like the authoritative knock of their landlady. So there was general surprise when Mrs. Flanagan opened the door. The fact was she could not repress the impulse to gratify her curiosity, which had been excited by the remarkably lavish dinner of her tenants.

"So I've caught you at dinner," she remarked, apologetically. "You must excuse me; it didn't occur to me that I might be intruding."

"It's of no consequence, Mrs. Flanagan," said Rose, not sorry, perhaps, that her old enemy should witness such an indication of prosperity. "I would invite you to dinner, but I am afraid there is no more of the turkey left."

"Roast turkey, upon my word! Well, here's luxury!" said Mrs. Flanagan. "I've had my supper, so I could not accept if you did invite me."

"We don't have turkey every day, Mrs. Flanagan," said Adeline. "We thought we would have it to-day by way of variety."

"They must have come into some money," thought Mrs. Flanagan. "Perhaps that old lady was their aunt."

"I'm sure I'm glad you're doin' so well," she said. "I hope you'll stay with me, in spite of all that's past and gone. You see I am that worried sometimes to get money to pay my rent that I may speak kind of cross like, but I don't mean anything—as is well known to you."

"Didn't you mean anything this morning when you were going to put us out of the house because I could not pay the whole of the rent?" asked Rose.

"I didn't mean it. They were only hasty words," said the landlady, stoutly. "I hope you'll stay with me, for it wouldn't look natural to see anybody else goin' in and comin' out of these rooms."

"I cannot tell yet what we may do," said Rose. "I am glad you didn't mean what you said this morning," she added, quietly, "for it made us feel very sober. I thought you meant to put us into the street."

"I'm sure I'm very sorry. I was cross, and I didn't know what I said. Well, I must be goin' down and gettin' Mike's supper, for he always comes home late."

"It's the way of the world, Rose," said Adeline, as the landlady disappeared.

"What does it all mean?" asked Harry, puzzled. "What has made that old cat so good-natured all at once?"

"Roast turkey," answered Rose, dryly. "She thinks we are prospering, and will be good tenants."

"You are going to stay, ain't you?"

Then the new prospects of the family were explained to Harry, who was much exhilarated by the account.

"Can't I give lessons in something?" he asked.

"You might give lessons in whistling," said Addie, who didn't enjoy her brother's performance in that line; "but I hope you won't receive pupils at home."

CHAPTER XX.

THE NEW HOME.

TWO days later Rose Beaufort received another call from Miss Jane Wilmot.

"My dear," said the spinster, "your new rooms are ready for you, and you can move in at once."

"Our rent is paid here till Saturday," suggested Rose.

"Give your landlady the benefit of the balance of the week. Is this furniture all yours?"

"Such as it is."

"You won't want it. Any articles that you do not value you had better send to an auction store to sell. The flat is already well furnished."

"A tenant on the floor below has offered to buy the furniture," said Rose.

"Does he make you a fair offer?"

"He offers thirty-five dollars."

"A low price, but it will save you trouble to accept it. When that matter is arranged I will send my carriage, and take you and your sister right over to your new home."

Without dwelling upon details, it is sufficient to say that before sunset the two sisters found themselves installed in a pretty and cosey home in a much better part of the city. There was a parlor, fronting on the street, a kitchen, and there were three sleeping-rooms, so that each of the little family could have one. The parlor contained a piano, a bookcase, well filled—this had not belonged to the recent tenants, but was supplied, without the knowledge of Rose, by Miss Wilmot.

Adeline uttered a cry of delight as she went from room to room.

"It is delightful!" she said.

"Here is an easy-chair for you," said Miss Wilmot. "It will be more comfortable than a rocking-chair, even."

This, too, had been added by the thoughtful spinster.

"Now open the piano and let me hear you play," said Miss Wilmot.

While Rose was playing, her benevolent friend nodded approvingly more than once.

"You'll do," she said. "I confess I had some doubts about your qualifications as a teacher, but I can see that you are a brilliant performer."

"If I can obtain pupils, I hope to suit," said Rose, modestly.

"I have some in view. An acquaintance of mine, Mrs. Tilton, of West Forty-second street, is in want of a music-teacher for her two girls. I will send you there, with a note, to-morrow. But first I must give you a hint. How much were you intending to charge for a lesson?"

"I had not thought," said Rose, hesitating. "How would fifty cents do?"

"Fifty cents!" repeated Miss Wilmot, with a rising inflection. "If you undervalue yourself to that extent, no one will think you know how to teach. You must charge two dollars per lesson."

"But will anybody pay me so much?" asked Rose, amazed. "To one who has only been earning thirty-five cents a day at vest-making, fifty cents an hour seems very large pay."

"My dear child, be guided by me. I know the world, and the world will set very much the same value upon you that you set on yourself. Ask Mrs. Tilton two dollars an hour."

"But if she objects to pay it?"

"Say that you are sorry that you cannot make any arrangements."

"I am afraid I can't keep a straight face when I ask such a price, Miss Wilmot."

"Oh, yes, you will! Don't feel nervous. If you lose the pupils, I will see that you don't suffer by it. By the way, put on your best dress, for it is desirable that you make a favorable first impression."

"I will follow your advice, Miss Wilmot," said Rose.

"You can't do better."

The next day Rose rang the bell at the door of a fine brown-stone house on West Forty-second street.

"Is Mrs. Tilton at home?" she asked.

"Yes, miss. Who shall I say wishes to see her?"

" The music-teacher."

Rose was shown into the drawing-room, and presently Mrs. Tilton entered. She was a tall, blonde lady of fashionable appearance, thoroughly worldly, and influenced by externals to a large extent.

" I believe Miss Wilmot has written you in reference to the subject of my call," said Rose.

" Yes, Miss Beaufort. You are a music-teacher?"

Rose bowed.

" My two little girls have made a beginning, but have only taken two quarters each. I wish them to have every advantage."

Rose bowed again.

" Of course, any one recommended by Miss Wilmot can hardly fail to be competent. May I ask, Miss Beaufort, where you live?"

" At the Wilmot Flats, in West Twenty-fifth street."

" Then you are a tenant of Miss Wilmot?"

" Yes, madam. My brother and sister and myself live together."

" Of course you have a piano at home?"

"Yes, madam," answered Rose, glad to answer the question in the affirmative.

"I asked because it might at times be more convenient—when we were preparing for company, for instance—to send your pupils to you."

"Just as may suit you, madam."

"Now, as to your terms, Miss Beaufort?"

"I charge two dollars per lesson," answered Rose, as boldly as she could.

"Isn't that high?" asked Mrs. Tilton. "Most lady teachers do not charge as much."

"I am quite aware of that," said Rose.

"I think some charge only a dollar per lesson."

"I presume you are right," said Rose; but, obedient to Miss Wilmot's suggestions, she didn't offer to reduce her own price. "I hope to make my services worth the amount I ask."

"Then you won't accept a less price?"

"I should prefer not to do so."

Mrs. Tilton was not a generous woman. She was disposed to haggle about prices, and had Rose applied to her for work as a seamstress she would have driven a hard bargain with her, but, as the friend and *protégé* of Miss Jane Wilmot, a lady of the highest social consideration, she did not venture to follow her own economical inclinations. In fact, Mrs. Tilton was not of an old family. Her husband had recently become rich, and though she aspired to be fashionable, there were circles to which she could not obtain admission. She plumed herself on her acquaintance with Miss Wilmot, and would not, on any account, have had Rose report to that lady that she had been unwilling to pay her price. Two dollars an hour seemed high, but she knew very well that she must buy social recognition, and that she valued above money.

"Very well," she said, after a pause; "I will pay your price. Can you give me Tuesday and Friday afternoons from three to five?"

"Yes, madam."

"Then we will commence next Tuesday, if you please. By the way, my neighbor, Mrs. Green, also desires to secure instruction for her daughter, and I promised to ask you to call."

"I will do so now if the lady is likely to be in," said Rose, gladly.

"I think you will find her in, now. You may hand her my card."

Mrs. Green lived but three doors away. She was at home, and engaged her, without any demur as to price, to give her daughter two hours a week, Monday and Thursday afternoons being selected.

As Rose walked home she could hardly credit her good fortune. Six lessons a week at two dollars apiece would amount to twelve dollars, and leave her plenty of time to herself. Twelve dollars! and till now her weekly income, laboring all day, had been less than three dollars.

"Addie," she said, after recounting her success to her sister, "do you know I feel quite like a young lady of fortune? I am almost afraid that it is all a dream, and that I shall wake up some day and find myself back again at Mrs. Flanagan's."

"Let us enjoy it as long as it lasts, Rose," said Adeline. "I wish I could help. I don't like to have the whole family leaning on you."

Adeline had her wish. Three days later Miss Wilmot came in with two little girls.

"They want to take lessons in drawing," she said. "They have a taste, but their father is a mechanic, and they have been unable to gratify it. Now, I have been thinking that I will let you pay the rent by instructing them, and leave your sister her whole time to teach music."

"I should like nothing better," said Adeline, brightening up.

"Then they will begin at once."

Adeline was fond of children, and found instruction in her favorite accomplishment no task, but a positive pleasure.

"I shall not be a burden upon you, Rose, any longer," she said, cheerfully.

"I should think not. If you pay the rent, it will be no light help. I shall insist in contributing my share, and will pay you fifteen dollars a month to make matters even."

Adeline protested, but Rose was firm. Her invalid sister's spirits were raised, and life was no longer monotonous, now that she felt herself of some use in the world.

" Do you know, Rose," she said, " I don't think I should be happier if our share of grandfather's money had come to us, as we once anticipated."

CHAPTER XXI.

THE COLLAPSE OF AN ELDERLY DUDE.

THE remarkable change that had taken place in the fortunes of Rose Beaufort interfered seriously with the plans of a person who has thus far only been incidentally mentioned—the superintendent of the work department of Nicholas Walton's large clothing store.

Hugh Parkinson was a man no longer young. If not forty, he looked that age. Moreover, his natural attractions, which were very scanty, had not been increased by the passage of time. His hair, which was of a reddish tinge, was carefully combed up from the side to cover the rather extensive vacancy for which time and irregular hours were responsible; but to look young was a problem which he had not been able to compass. He did what he could, in the way of dress, to make up for the ravages of time. He always got his clothes made by a fashionable Broadway tailor, and in the street he looked like an elderly "dude," and thus far more ridiculous than the younger specimens of this class.

Perhaps it is well for our self-conceit that we do not see ourselves as others see us. Hugh Parkinson, when he surveyed himself in the mirror, decided that he was handsome and stylish-looking. He felt that it was time he married. His salary was a liberal one—fifty dollars per week—and he had a snug sum in various savings banks, representing the savings of the last ten years.

"I'm a good catch!" he said to himself, complacently; "I've a right to expect considerable in a wife. Egad! I must be getting married while I am still a young man."

He had been a young man for a good many years, and so entitled to call himself such.

Hugh Parkinson was fastidious, however, and he had never met the one he wanted to marry till he saw Rose Beaufort. Rose was about half his age, and her fresh beauty touched the heart—such as he had—of the old young man.

"She has no fortune, but what does that matter?" he said to himself, magnanimously. "I have enough for both. When she goes with me to the theatre she will excite the admiration of all, and all the young men in society will envy me. Egad! I must marry her."

Rose, however, had as yet shown no signs of admiring Mr. Parkinson. Indeed, the superintendent had good reason to doubt whether she even esteemed him. He saw, however, that she was poor. Marriage with him would bring her comfort, and even a moderate degree of luxury; upon this he depended for a favorable issue to his suit. As to her being poor, that was evident enough. To be sure, she was well dressed, but no one who is in good circumstances takes vests to make at thirty-five cents apiece. Besides, he knew where she lived, for the vest-makers were obliged to leave their addresses with their names; and he had passed through Bleecker street, and seen for himself the shabby tenement-house in which Rose lived.

"I wish she might become poorer still,"

said Mr. Parkinson to himself; "then I would
have a chance to step in as her good angel
and relieve her from suffering. She couldn't
help being drawn to me."

When Rose called and desired pay for the
two vests which she had completed, Mr. Parkinson was pleased; it showed that she was becoming harder pressed by poverty.

"Daniells," he said to the examining clerk,
"when Miss Beaufort calls with her package
of vests I want you to object to the quality of
her work."

"But, Mr. Parkinson, her work is always
well done," objected Daniells.

"Oh, well, you can always find faults.
Just say that she must see me before you feel
authorized to pay her."

"What's your game, Mr. Parkinson?"
asked Daniells.

Mr. Parkinson winked significantly.

"The fact is, Daniells," he said, "I want
an opportunity to ingratiate myself with the
fair Rose. I will take her part, pay her the
money as a favor, and—you comprehend?"

"Yes, I see. The fact is, Rose is pretty,

and if I were not a married man I would try to obtain a smile from her myself."

"Just do as I tell you, there's a good fellow, and you won't lose by it."

When Rose had obtained by good fortune the powerful friendship of the rich Miss Wilmot, she, of course, decided to give up vest-making. She had some time left, but she felt that it would be necessary for her to keep up her practice at home, if she aspired to become a successful piano-teacher. However, she would finish the vests she had in hand, and let those be the last.

When the vests were finished she took them round to Mr. Walton's establishment.

The vigilant Daniells did not fail to note her appearance, and prepared to serve the interests of his superior in the way which had been arranged between them.

"So you've finished the vests?" he said, carelessly. "Let me look at them."

Rose regarded this as a mere formality, knowing that they had been well made, and never before having had her work objected to.

What was her surprise, therefore, when

Daniells went over them one by one, frowning and shaking his head, disapprovingly.

"Really," he said, "these vests are hardly satisfactory."

"What is amiss with them?" asked Rose, in genuine surprise.

"I can't go into particulars," said Daniells, who would have found it hard to do so, by the way; "I can only say that they are not as well made as we expect."

"They are as well made as usual," said Rose, flushing indignantly. "I cannot understand why you object to them, when all the work I've done before has passed without objection."

"All I can say, Miss Beaufort, is that I do not feel authorized to pay you for them. Mr. Parkinson, however, is my superior. You can refer the matter to him."

"I should like to do so, sir," said Rose, with cold dignity.

"I will accompany you."

The two passed on to the superintendent's desk, and Daniells explained the matter to his superior.

"I will look over the work myself," said Parkinson. "You may go back, Mr. Daniells. I will settle the matter."

Rose stood quiet, while the superintendent examined the vests.

"Really, Miss Beaufort," said Hugh, with his fascinating smile, "I think Mr. Daniells has done you injustice. To my eye, the vests are very neatly made."

"Thank you, sir," said Rose, gratefully. "I am sure they are as well made as any I have brought here."

"The fact is," said Parkinson, confidentially, "Daniells is rather fussy—I might say cranky—I have had more than once to reverse his decision. You shall certainly be paid promptly, as usual."

"Thank you, sir."

Rose had never admired the superintendent, but he seemed to her now a just and agreeable man. The money was not now of so much importance to her, but she strongly objected to being unjustly treated, and being deprived of the money which she had fairly earned.

Mr. Parkinson himself paid over to Rose the money due for the six vests.

"Miss Beaufort," he said, "I hope you won't think we men of business are all hard and disposed to take advantage of the poor. Now, in your case, I assure you that I feel very kindly toward you."

"Thank you, sir," said Rose, considerably surprised.

Mr. Parkinson's vanity led him to think that she was regarding him with a look of interest, but he misinterpreted her. She looked upon him as old enough to be her father, and not a suspicion had ever entered her mind that he thought of her as a possible wife.

"If you will permit me," said the superintendent, "I am about to go out to lunch, and will communicate to you a plan I have for your advantage. It will be better not to take any new work now."

"I did not intend to," said Rose.

Mr. Parkinson looked a little surprised.

They passed through the store together, and out into Broadway. Rose waited for Mr.

Parkinson to say what he appeared to have in his mind.

"I think, Miss Beaufort," he said, as they emerged into the street, "you could do better than make vests at thirty-five cents each."

"I think so, too," answered Rose. "I wonder what he means?" she thought.

"Such a beautiful girl as you are——"

"Sir!" exclaimed Rose, haughtily.

"No offense, my dear. Quite the contrary, I assure you. I have had my eye upon you for some time, and I admire you exceedingly. You are poor, but I shall overlook that. My dear girl, I am very well off, as you may suppose, and I offer to make you Mrs. Parkinson."

"Good-evening, sir," said Rose, coldly. "I don't wish to continue the conversation."

"Don't be foolish, my dear girl. It is a fine chance for a poor vest-maker to marry a man in my position."

Rose did not deign to answer, but tried to escape. He attempted to seize her by the arm, when his hat was violently knocked over his eyes, and he came near measuring his length on the sidewalk.

CHAPTER XXII.

THE ROMANCE OF A ROSE.

MR. PARKINSON adjusted his hat, and darted a glance of indignation at a fine-looking young man who had come to the rescue of Rose Beaufort.

"This is an outrage, sir," he said, angrily.

Clinton Randall paid no attention to the discomfited Parkinson, but asked Rose:

"Has this man annoyed you?"

"He forced his attentions upon me," answered Rose.

"If he has insulted you, I will take care that he is punished."

"Don't meddle with what is none of your business," said Parkinson, furiously. "I have a good mind to horsewhip you."

"Make the attempt whenever you please, sir," said Randall, significantly. "If ever I find you annoying this young lady again, I shall probably give you a taste of the same medicine."

"Annoying?" sneered Parkinson. "I offered to make her my wife, if you call that annoyance. Let me tell you that when a gentleman in my position offers to marry a vest-maker she has reason to feel complimented."

"She evidently does not," said Randall, not without sarcasm. "Whether she is a vest-maker or not, she is evidently a young lady, and is entitled to be treated as such."

"She will be sorry for having made such a fuss," said Parkinson, spitefully. "Miss Beaufort," he continued, turning to Rose, "you need not trouble yourself to come to the store again for work, as I shall decline to give you any. You may regret having treated me with such scant courtesy."

"I had no intention of asking for more work," said Rose, coldly.

"Perhaps you have come into a fortune," sneered Parkinson.

"Enough of this!" said Randall, sternly. "This young lady has no favors to ask of

you. You had better go back to your master
and conduct yourself hereafter in a more becoming manner, or you may repent it."

Here was a fresh outrage for poor Parkinson. In his own eyes he was a man of very
great importance, and to be told by this young
man, before a common vest-maker, to go back
to his master, was very humiliating. He was
trying to think of some scathing retort, when
Randall, with a bow, offered his arm to Rose,
and they walked away together.

"I wonder whether she really doesn't care
for any more work," thought Parkinson, "or
is it only pretense? I dare say she will, after
a while, be coming round again for vests to
make. If she does, I shall have her in my
power."

And the superintendent walked slowly back
to the store, chafing inwardly at his ill-suc-
cess.

"I hope you won't allow yourself to think
of this disagreeable occurrence," said Clinton
Randall, "or of this unmannerly cur."

"No, sir, thanks to your kindness, I shall
have no occasion."

"He seemed spiteful. I hope it is not in his power to annoy you."

He said this, thinking that Rose might be dependent upon Parkinson for work.

"Last week he might have done so," answered Rose. "I was engaged in making vests for the store in which he is employed, and he might have refused me work. Now, fortunately, thanks to a kind lady, I have no further occasion to apply to him."

"I am heartily glad to hear it. Any connection with such a cur must be disagreeable. Has he ever annoyed you before?"

"Never; and I was much surprised to-day when he followed me from the store and pressed his attentions upon me."

"He is old enough to be your father—the old fool!" said Randall, resentfully.

It seemed to him profanation that such a man should have thought of appropriating the fresh beauty of the charming girl at his side.

"He thought I ought to regard myself honored by his proposal," said Rose, smiling, as she thought of the unromantic figure of her elderly lover.

"He has found out by this time that you hold a different opinion. If he should ever persecute you again, I hope I may be at hand to rescue you once more."

"I am not likely to meet him, and have no further occasion to make vests for a living. If you will kindly stop the next up-town car, I will not longer detain you."

"Certainly," answered Randall; and as a car was just at hand, he complied with her request.

He stood on the sidewalk, following, with his glances, the Broadway car into which he had helped Rose.

"I wish I dare follow her, and find out who she is," said Randall to himself; "but she might misinterpret my motive and class me with that elderly reprobate with whom I was compelled to interfere. What a charming girl she is! I never saw a sweeter expression, or a more beautiful complexion."

He was in a day-dream, from which he was presently roused.

"What are you staring at, Randall?" asked a young man of about his own age, slapping him on the shoulder. "You seem star-gazing."

"So I am."

"Star-gazing at midday?"

"It is a human star, Tudor. In short, it is a beautiful girl, whom I have just helped into a car."

"Who is she?"

"I don't know, I'm sure."

"An unknown divinity, eh? Tell me about it, for there is evidently a story under all this."

"A very short one. I found an elderly scamp annoying her, and knocked his hat over his eyes."

"And, after having gallantly rescued her, you helped her into a car?"

"Exactly."

"And that is the whole of it?"

"I am afraid so."

"You don't mean to say you are struck at last, Randall—you who have so long been the despair of manœuvering mammas? Come, that would be news, indeed!"

"I am not at all sure but I am. Tudor, I

will say one thing, that I never saw a sweeter face in all my wanderings."

"That's saying a good deal, for you have been all over the world. And you don't know the young lady's name?"

"Haven't the slightest clew to it."

"Is she rich or poor, a stylish city lady or a rustic beauty?"

"I fancy she is not rich," said Randall, who, for some reason, did not care to mention that she had been a vest-maker. To him it mattered little, but his friend Tudor might be more fastidious, and he was not willing to give him any chance to look down upon Rose.

"Couldn't you manage to ask her name?"

Randall shook his head.

"I tried to think of a pretext, but could not," he answered.

"You may meet her again."

"I hope to do so."

"And if you do?"

Randall smiled.

"Considering that it is not over ten minutes since I first set eyes upon her, it is, perhaps, a little premature to consider that question. I shall certainly try to meet her again."

The two young men sauntered up-town, and the conversation fell upon other themes, but Clinton Randall seemed unusually thoughtful. Do what he might, he could not help recurring again and again to the fair face which he had seen for the first time that morning.

When Rose was at home again the matter seemed no longer serious to her. Whenever she thought of Mr. Parkinson and his suit she felt inclined to laugh.

"Addie," she said, "I have had a proposal this morning."

"A proposal!" repeated her sister, in surprise.

"Yes, an offer of marriage."

"You are not in earnest?"

"Indeed I am! I am not sure but I shall give you a brother-in-law."

"I wasn't aware that you knew any eligible young man."

"He isn't a young man. Let me describe him to you. His name is Parkinson; he is somewhere between forty and fifty; he is par-

tially bald, and—I am not quite sure that he
is not bow-legged."

"And you love him?" queried Adeline,
mischievously. "If so, I give my consent,
for though I had hoped for a better-looking
brother-in-law, I am not willing that your
young affections should be blighted."

"Nonsense, Addie," returned Rose, half-
vexed.

"Tell me all about it."

Rose did so, and her sister listened with
fixed interest.

"And this young man who rescued you,
and knocked your adorer's hat over his eyes.
I suppose he was a commonplace young man,
red-haired and freckled, perhaps?"

"Indeed he was not," said Rose, indignantly.

"Then he was handsome?"

"Yes, I think that he would be considered
so."

"Take care you don't dream of him. It
would be very romantic—wouldn't it?—if
you should marry him, as generally happens
in romances."

"Don't be a goose, Addie!" said Rose; but she did not seem annoyed. Secretly, she thought Clinton Randall the most attractive young man she had ever met, and wondered if fate would ever throw them together again.

CHAPTER XXIII.

ON THE BORDERS OF THE LAKE OF GENEVA.

IT is time to look after our hero in his European wanderings.

He had been travelling hither and thither with his guardian, who appeared to have no definite aim except to enjoy himself. Whether he succeeded in doing this was by no means certain. On the whole, he and Ben got along very well together. He did not undertake to control his young secretary, but left him very much to his own devices. There were times when he seemed irritable, but it generally happened when he had been losing money at the gaming-table, for he was fond of play, not so much because he was fascinated by it as because it served as a distraction in lieu of more serious pursuits. On the whole, he did not lose much, for he was cool and self-possessed.

One thing was unsatisfactory to Ben—he had little or nothing to do. He was private secretary in name, but what use Major Grafton had for a private secretary Ben could not divine.

Why Ben need have concerned himself, as long as he received his salary, may excite the wonder of some of my readers, but I think most people like to feel that they are doing something useful.

Ben, however, found a use for part of his time. In his travels through France, Switzerland, and Italy, he had oftentimes found himself, when alone, at a loss on account of a want of knowledge of the French language.

"Why should I not learn it?" he asked himself.

He procured some elementary French books, including a grammar, dictionary, and tourist's guide, and set himself to the task with his usual energy. Having little else to do, he made remarkable progress, and found his studies a source of great interest.

"What are you doing there, Philip?" asked Major Grafton, one afternoon.

"I am trying to obtain some knowledge of French. I suppose you have no objection?"

"Not the least in the world. Do you want a teacher?"

"No, sir; I think I can get along by myself."

Major Grafton was rather glad that Ben had found some way of passing his time. He did not want the boy to become homesick, for his presence was important to him for reasons that we are acquainted with.

Ben supplemented his lessons by going into shops, pricing articles, and attempting to hold a conversation with the clerks. This was a practical way of learning the language, which he found of great use.

Again they found themselves in Geneva, which Ben thought, on the whole, a pleasant place of residence. Here, too, he could make abundant use of his new acquisition, and did not fail to avail himself of his opportunity. So he enjoyed his stay in the charming Swiss city until one day he made an astounding discovery.

The most interesting walk in Geneva is

along the borders of the lake. Near it are placed seats on which the visitor may sit and survey the unequalled view.

Ben had seated himself one day, with a French book in his hand, which he was studying, when he observed a couple of ladies seat themselves near him. He would have given them no further thought if by chance the name of Major Grafton, spoken by one of them, had not reached his ears.

"I see that Major Grafton is here," said one. "You know we met him at Florence."

"Yes, the one who had the sick boy with him."

"The same."

"It was his son, was it not?"

"I thought so at the time, but I have since learned that I was mistaken. He was the boy's guardian."

"The boy died, did he not?"

"Yes, and it must have been a serious calamity to him."

"You mean that he was very much attached to the boy?"

"No, I don't mean that. On the contrary,

he appeared to care very little for him. It was the pecuniary loss I was thinking of."

" Explain yourself."

" You must know, then, that the boy was heir to a large fortune, the income of which, during his minority, was payable to Major Grafton for his benefit. No doubt the guardian made a good thing out of it. He probably made it pay both the boy's expenses and his own."

" Then, on the boy's death, he would lose this income ?"

" Precisely."

" It is strange," said the younger lady; " but he still has a boy with him."

" He has ?" inquired the other, in surprise.

" The name he calls him is Philip."

"That was the name of the boy who died."

" Are you sure that he died? Are you sure that this is not the same boy ?"

" Positive."

" It is very singular. A strange idea has occurred to me."

" What is it ?"

" What if he is passing off this boy for the

first, in order to retain the liberal income which he received as guardian?"

" But that would be fraudulent."

" That is true; but I think Major Grafton would be capable of it. I hear from my brother that he gambles, and a gambler is not apt to be overburdened with principle."

"If this is so, he ought to be exposed. To whom would the boy's fortune go, if it were known that he was dead?"

" To three cousins, who, I understand, are living in poverty in New York. There are two young girls and a brother, named Beaufort. They were cut off by the grandfather, from whom the fortune was inherited. For what reason I am not aware. However, the will stipulated that if the boy should die, the fortune should go to these children."

" Then they ought to be enjoying it now?"

" Exactly. If all is true that I suspect, they are being kept out of it by a conspiracy."

" Who is the boy that Major Grafton has with him now?"

" I don't know. Possibly it is a relative of

his own. He calls him Philip to deceive the public, if all is as I suspect."

"Don't you think we ought to do something in the matter, Clara?"

"I never meddle with matters that don't concern me."

"Not even to right such a wrong as this?"

"No; I suppose matters will come right after awhile. The deception will be discovered, you may depend upon it."

"If I knew the boy I would speak to him about it."

"You would have your labor for your pains. The boy is probably in the conspiracy. I think he is a nephew of Major Grafton. If anything were said to him, he would no doubt put the major on his guard, and that would be the end of it. My dear, we shall do much better not to interfere in the matter at all."

The younger lady looked dissatisfied, but did not reply.

The feelings with which Ben heard this revelation may be imagined. He never for a moment doubted the truth of the story. It made clear to him what had seemed singular hitherto. He had never been able to understand why Major Grafton should pick him up, and without any inquiry into his capacity offer him an engagement as private secretary. He had found that the office was merely nominal, and that there were no duties to speak of connected with it. Major Grafton had shown no particular interest in him, and evidently cared nothing for him, save as he served his purpose. But if his presence enabled Grafton to remain in possession of a large income, there was no need to inquire further. Ben saw that he was made an important agent in a wicked conspiracy to divert a large fortune from its lawful owners.

What ought he to do?

CHAPTER XXIV.

THE MAISON DE FOUS.

THIS question of what he ought to do
disturbed Ben not a little. As an honorable boy he did not wish to benefit any
longer than was absolutely necessary by a
deception which involved injustice and fraud.
He was living very comfortably, it is true,
and his allowance was a handsome one. He
sent half of it to his mother, and this was
sufficient to provide all that was needed for
her and his sister's comfort. He had done
this innocently, hitherto, but now that his
eyes were opened, his knowledge would make
him an accomplice in the conspiracy.

In his uncertainty he decided upon what
was not, perhaps, the most judicious course, to
ask Major Grafton directly in regard to the
matter.

An opportunity soon came.

"Major Grafton," Ben began, "how long since did Philip die?"

The major regarded him suspiciously. The question put him on his guard.

"A few months ago," he answered indifferently.

"Were you—his guardian?"

"You seem curious this morning, Philip," answered the major, coldly.

If Ben had been older and more experienced he would have been able to get at the truth indirectly, but it was his nature to be straightforward.

"I heard something yesterday that disturbed me," he said.

Major Grafton threw himself back in an easy-chair and fixed his eyes searchingly on the boy.

"Tell me what you heard," he said, shortly, "and from whom."

"I was sitting on a bench near the lake when two ladies began speaking about you—and me."

"Tell me what they said," broke in Grafton, impatiently.

14

"The truth must be told," thought Ben, "even if Major Grafton gets offended."

"They said that Philip had a large fortune, and you were his guardian. When he died the money was to go to some cousins in New York. They said that you had concealed his death, and so continued to draw the income of the property, and were palming off me for him. They seemed to think I was your nephew, and was in the plot."

Major Grafton was a good deal disturbed by what Ben had told him. Of course there was a strong chance that the truth would come out some time, but he had hoped to keep it concealed for some years, perhaps.

"These ladies seem to have a large share of imagination," he said, with a forced laugh. "From one fabrication you may judge all. You know whether you are my nephew or not, and whether you are engaged in any plot?"

"No, sir, of course not."

"The whole thing is ridiculous; I don't think you need trouble yourself any more about it."

But Ben was not satisfied, and Major Grafton could see this from his look.

"That was my reason for asking whether Philip had any property," he continued, with an inquiring look.

"I must satisfy him in some way," thought the major, "or he will compromise me."

"I wouldn't like to think I was keeping any property away from the rightful owners," proceeded Ben.

"You can put yourself at ease," said the major, carelessly. "Those ladies, whoever they are, know almost nothing about the matter. Philip did have a little property, yielding scarcely enough for his own expenses. At his death it fell to me. His grandfather was an intimate friend of mine, and made the arrangement in gratitude for my care of the boy."

"Then there were no cousins in New York?" asked Ben, doubtfully.

"Not that I am aware of. That is a lie out of whole cloth. There is no one more unscrupulous than a female gossip. Did you speak to either of the ladies?"

" No, sir."

"That was right. You might have made mischief and seriously offended me. Do you often write home?"

" Every week, sir."

" I have no objection to that, but I must caution you against repeating this nonsensical and absurd story. I have taken a great deal of interest in you on account of your resemblance to poor Philip, to whom I was tenderly attached. It is on that account I engaged you to accompany me. You would not be likely to do as well in New York?"

" No, sir; no one would think of paying me as liberally as you do."

" I am glad you appreciate the advantages of your position. I hope you won't lose it by any foolishness," added Grafton, significantly.

Ben felt that there was no more to say, but he was far from satisfied. He was thoroughly persuaded within himself that the story was true, and that Major Grafton was acting a fraudulent part. How could he find out?

He had not forgotten his visit to the office of Mr. Codicil, just before they left New

York. He had seen enough, then, to be aware that between Major Grafton and the lawyer there were business relations, and he suspected that they referred to the boy whose place he had taken. This would seem to bear out and confirm the story told by the two ladies. Now, if he should write a letter to Mr. Codicil he might ascertain all he needed to know, and if all was as he suspected he could refuse having any further part in the conspiracy. He did not remember the exact location of Mr. Codicil's office, but he did remember his first name, and he judged rightly that a letter simply directed to the lawyer, and addressed New York, would be likely to reach him.

Major Grafton, after the interview between Ben and himself, watched our hero with ever-increasing suspicion. He felt that he was in the boy's power. An indiscreet revelation would overthrow the fabric of fraud which in his self-interest he had erected, and reduce him to earning a precarious living at the gaming-table. In the case of an average boy he would have been secure, from the boy's regard for his own interest; but he saw that Ben was a conscientious boy, of honorable impulses, and this disgusted him.

"The boy is dangerous," he decided. "I must place him where he can do no mischief."

. When a man is thoroughly unprincipled he can always find ways and means for the carrying out of his iniquitous plans. Major Grafton experienced no difficulty in devising a method for staving off the threatened danger.

One day after a leisurely breakfast, during which Major Grafton had been unusually chatty and affable, he said:

"Philip, I have a pleasure in store for you."

"What is it, sir?"

"We are going to take a long drive into the country."

"Thank you, sir. I shall enjoy it."

Fifteen minutes afterward an open carriage drove into the court-yard of the hotel.

"Is this the carriage I ordered?" asked Major Grafton.

"It is for M. de Grafton," said the driver.

" But you are not the man I spoke to."

" No, it was my brother. He is obliged to stay at home; his wife is taken suddenly sick."

" Very well; you will no doubt answer the purpose equally well. Philip, take a seat inside."

Ben did so.

" Where shall I drive, monsieur?"

Major Grafton indicated the direction.

They drove over a broad, smooth road on the eastern shore of the lake. It was a charming drive, not alone on account of the smooth waters of the lake which were in constant view, but also on account of the distant mountains and the picturesque Swiss habitations which regaled their eyes.

They kept on uninterruptedly for nearly two hours, until Ben began to marvel at the length of the drive.

Finally they came in sight of a large, picturesquely situated house, surrounded by trees.

" We will descend here, Philip," said Major Grafton. " I want you to see this chateau."

"Is there anything interesting connected with it?" asked Ben.

"Yes, I believe Voltaire once lived here," answered Grafton.

"I always thought he lived at the Chateau de Ferney."

"He also lived here for a few months," said Major Grafton, shortly. "I think Calvin also lived here once."

Ben entered without suspicion. A suave, black-whiskered man welcomed them. He seemed to recognize Major Grafton, and was voluble in his protestations of joy at meeting them.

"Is this the boy you spoke of?" he asked.

"Yes," answered Grafton. "Philip," he said, "remain in this room a few minutes while I speak with M. Bourdon."

"Certainly, sir."

He waited fifteen, twenty, thirty minutes, and no one came back. Finally the door opened and the black-whiskered man made his appearance—alone.

"Where is Major Grafton?" asked Ben.

The other smiled craftily.

" He is gone, M. Philippe."

" Gone! and without me?"

" You are to live with me, my son."

" I don't understand you. What sort of a place is this?"

" It is a *maison de fous.*"

Ben was horror-struck. He knew now that he was in a lunatic asylum. He could guess why he was placed there.

CHAPTER XXV.

IN A TRAP.

FOR a sane person to find himself suddenly incarcerated in a lunatic asylum is enough to excite a thrill of horror in the most stolid. Ben shuddered and started back, pale and sick with apprehension. He was a brave boy, but it required more courage than he possessed to preserve his coolness under such circumstances.

"What does it mean?" he ejaculated.

"It means, my friend," answered M. Bourdon, with a sardonic smile, "that you are not quite right here," and he tapped his forehead significantly.

He spoke English correctly, but with an accent, having, when a young man, passed several years in England.

"It is a lie!" exclaimed Ben, indignantly, his terror giving place to anger. "My mind is not in the least affected."

M. Bourdon shrugged his shoulders, with another aggravating smile.

"They all say so," he answered.

"I am as sane as you are!" continued Ben, hotly.

"Well, well, I may be a little touched my-self—who knows?" said M. Bourdon, or the doctor, as we may call him, in a tone of banter.

It was hard for Ben to restrain himself, so impressed was he by the outrage of which he was the victim. It would have been a relief to attack the doctor, and seek deliverance by forcible means, but a glance at the well-knit frame of M. Bourdon, and the certainty of his being able to summon assistance, deterred him and led him to control his rash impulse. One thing he could do, and that was to ascertain, if possible, Major Grafton's motive in subjecting him to imprisonment.

"What proof have you that I am insane?" he asked, more calmly.

"Your appearance."

"You have not had time to examine me."

"The doctors are able to judge from

very slight examination," said M. Bourdon, smiling.

"Did Major Grafton tell you I was insane?" asked Ben.

"You mean the gentleman who came here with you?"

"Yes."

"He has assured me of it."

"What did he say? How did he tell you I had shown signs of insanity?"

"He said you had tried to drown yourself in the lake, and, being foiled in that, had made an attempt to poison him. Surely this is enough to warrant his sending you to me."

"Did he utter these infamous falsehoods?" demanded Ben, startled.

"Of course you pronounce them falsehoods, my young friend, and doubtless you believe what you say. I am quite sure you have no recollection of what you did. This is one of your sane periods. At this moment you are as sane as I am."

"You admit that?" said Ben, in surprise.

"Certainly, for it is true. Your insanity

is fitful—paroxysmal. Half an hour hence you may stand in need of a strait-jacket. If you were always as clear in mind as at present there would be no need of detaining you. I would open my door and say, ' Go, my young friend. You do not need my care.' Unfortunately, we do not know how long this mood may last."

The doctor spoke smoothly and plausibly, and it was hard for Ben to tell whether he was really in earnest or not. He regarded M. Bourdon intently, and thought he detected a slight mocking smile, which excited his doubt and distrust anew. To appeal to such a man seemed well-nigh hopeless, but there was nothing else to do.

"Are you the doctor?" he asked.

"Yes; I am Dr. Bourdon," was the reply.

"And you are at the head of this establishment?" continued Ben.

"I have that honor, my young friend," answered Bourdon.

"Then I wish to tell you that Major Grafton has deceived you. He has an object to serve in having me locked up here."

"Doubtless," answered the doctor, with an amused smile, taking a pinch of snuff.

"He is afraid I would reveal a secret which would strip him of his income," continued Ben.

"And that secret is——?" said the doctor, not without curiosity.

Ben answered this question as briefly and clearly as he could.

The doctor listened with real interest, and it might have been satisfactory to Ben had he known that his story was believed. M. Bourdon was a shrewd man of the world, and it struck him that this knowledge might enable him to demand more extortionate terms of Major Grafton.

"Don't you believe me?" asked Ben, watching the face of his listener.

"I hear a great many strange stories," said the doctor. "I have to be cautious about what I believe."

"But surely you will believe me, knowing that I am perfectly sane?"

"That is the question to be determined," said M. Bourdon, smiling.

"Won't you investigate it?" pleaded Ben. "It is a crime to keep me here, when I am of sound mind."

"Whenever I am convinced of that I will let you go. Meanwhile you must be quiet, and submit to the rules of my establishment."

"How long do you expect to keep me here?" asked Ben.

"As long as you require it and your board is paid."

Ben looked despondent, for this assurance held out very little hope of release. Still he was young, and youth is generally hopeful. Something might turn up. Ben was determined that something should turn up. He was not going to remain shut up in a madhouse any longer than he could help. He remained silent, and M. Bourdon touched a little bell upon a small table beside the door.

The summons was answered by a stout man with rough, black locks, who looked like a hotel porter.

"Francois," said the doctor, in the French language, "conduct this young man to No. 19."

"At once, *Monsieur le Docteur*," answered the attendant. "Come with me, young man."

He signed to Ben to follow him, and our hero, realizing the utter futility of resistance, did so.

"Go ahead, monsieur," said Francois, when they came to a staircase.

Ben understood him very well, though he spoke in French, thanks to his assiduous study of the last four weeks.

They walked along a narrow corridor, and Francois, taking from his pocket a bunch of keys, carefully selected one and opened the door.

" *Entrez, monsieur.*"

Ben found himself in an apartment about the size of a hall bedroom, with one window, and a narrow bedstead, covered with an exceedingly thin mattress. There was no carpet on the floor, and the furniture was very scanty. It consisted of but one chair, a cheap bureau, and a washstand. And this was to be Ben's home—for how long?

"I must get acquainted with this man,"

thought Ben. " I must try to win his good-will, and perhaps he may be able to help me to escape."

"Is your name Francois?" he asked, as the man lingered at the door.

" *Oui, monsieur.*"

" And how long have you been here—in this asylum ?"

"How long, monsieur? Five years, nearly."

" There is some mistake about my being here, Francois. I don't look crazy, do I ?"

" No, monsieur ; but——"

" But what ?"

" That proves nothing."

" There is a plot against me, and I am put here by an enemy. I want you to be my friend. Here, take this."

Ben produced from his pocket a silver franc piece and offered it to Francois, who took it eagerly, for the man's besetting sin was avarice.

" Thanks, monsieur—much thanks !" he said, his stolid face lighting up. " I will be a friend."

" Francois !"

At the call from below Francois hastily thrust the coin into his pocket, nodded significantly to Ben, and, retiring, locked the door behind him.

CHAPTER XXVI.

INTRODUCES TWO CELEBRITIES.

WHAT a change a short half-hour may make in the position and feelings of any person! Little did Ben imagine, when he set out on a drive in the morning with Major Grafton, that he was on his way to one of the most hopeless of prisons.

It was hard even now for him to realize his position. He looked from the window, and with a glance of envy saw in a field, not far away, some Swiss peasants at work. They were humble people, living a quiet, uneventful, laborious life; yet Ben felt that they were infinitely better off than he, provided he were doomed to pass the remainder of his life in this refuge. But of this he would not entertain the idea. He was young, not yet seventeen, and life was full of pleasant possibilities.

"I am a Yankee," he thought, "and I

don't believe they will succeed in keeping me here long. I will keep a bright lookout for a chance to escape."

Half an hour later Ben heard the key grate in the lock, and, fixing his eyes on the entrance, he saw Francois enter.

"Monsieur, dinner is ready," he said.

Ben, notwithstanding his disagreeable situation, felt that he, too, was ready for the dinner. He was glad to find that it was not to be served to him in his own room. He would have a chance of seeing the other inmates of the house.

"Where is it?" he asked.

"Follow me," answered Francois, of course in French.

He led the way, and Ben followed him into a lower room, long and narrow, which was used as the dining-room. There were no side-windows, and it would have been quite dark but for a narrow strip of window near the ceiling.

Around a plain table sat a curious collection of persons. It was easy to see that something was the matter with them, for I do not

wish to have it understood that all the inmates of the house were, like our hero, perfectly sane. M. Bourdon was not wholly a
quack, but he was fond of money, and, looking through the eyes of self-interest, he was
willing to consider Ben insane, although he
knew very well that he was as rational as
himself.

"Sit here, monsieur," said Francois.

Ben took the seat indicated, and naturally
turned to survey his immediate neighbors.

The one on the right-hand was a tall, ven-
erable-looking man, with white hair and a
flowing beard, whose manner showed the most
perfect decorum. The other was a thin, dark-
complexioned man, of bilious aspect, and
shifty, evasive eyes. Neither noticed Ben at
first, as the dinner appeared to engross their
first attention. This consisted of a thin broth
and a section of a loaf of coarse bread as the
first course. Ben had been accustomed to
more luxurious fare, and he was rather surprised to see with what enjoyment his neighbors partook of it. Next came a plate of
meat, and this was followed by a small por-

tion of grapes. There was nothing more. It was clear that M. Bourdon did not consider rich fare good for his patients.

"I think I would rather dine at the hotel," thought Ben; but the diet was not by any means the worst thing of which he complained.

"If I were free I would not mind how poor and plain my fare was," he thought.

His companions finished dinner before him, and had leisure to bestow some attention upon him.

"My little gentleman, do you come from Rome?" asked the venerable old gentleman on his right.

"No, sir," answered Ben.

"I am sorry. I wished to ask you a question."

"Indeed, sir. Perhaps I might answer it even now. I have been in Florence."

"No; that will not do; and yet, perhaps you may have met persons coming from Rome?"

"I did, monsieur."

"Then perhaps they told you how things were going on."

"Very well, I believe, monsieur."

"No, that could not be," said the old gentleman, shaking his head. "I am sure nothing would go well without me."

"Do you, then, live in Rome?" asked Ben, curiously.

"Surely!" exclaimed the old man. "Did you not know that the Pope lived in Rome?"

"But what has that to do with you, sir?"

"A great deal. Know, my little gentleman, that I—to whom you are speaking—am the Pope."

This was said with an air of importance.

"There's no doubt about his being insane," thought Ben.

"How, then, do you happen to be here?" asked our hero, interested to see what his companion would say.

"I was abducted," said the old gentleman, lowering his voice, "by an emissary of the King of America. M. Bourdon is a cousin of the king, and he is in the plot. But they won't keep me here long."

"I hope not," said Ben, politely.

"The King of Spain has promised to send

an army to deliver me. I only received his letter last week. You will not tell M. Bourdon, will you?"

"Certainly not," answered Ben.

"It is well; I thought I could rely upon your honor."

"My friend," said another voice, that of his left-hand neighbor, "you are losing your time in talking with that old fool. The fact is, he isn't right here," and he touched his head.

The Pope appeared deeply absorbed in thought, and did not hear this complimentary remark.

"He thinks he is the Pope. He is no more the Pope than I am."

Ben nodded non-committally.

"He ought to be here. But I—I am the victim of an infamous horde of enemies, who have placed me here."

"Why should they do that, sir?"

"To keep me out of my rights. It is the English Government that has done it. Of course, you know who I am."

"No, sir, I don't think I do."

"Look well at me!" and the dark man threw himself back in his chair for inspection.

"I am afraid I don't recognize you, monsieur," said Ben.

"Bah! where are your eyes?" said the other, contemptuously. "I am Napoleon Bonaparte!"

"But I thought you died at St. Helena," said Ben.

"Quite a mistake, I assure you. The English Government so asserted, but it was a deception. They wished my memory to die out among my faithful French. They buried my effigy, but smuggled me off in a vessel late at night. They placed me here, and here they mean to keep me—if they can. But some day I shall escape; I shall re-enter France; I shall summon all to my banner, and at the head of a great army I shall enter Paris. Do you know what I will do then?"

"What will you do, sir?" asked Ben, with some curiosity.

"I shall descend upon England with an army of five millions of men," said the dark man, his eyes flashing, "and burn all her cities and towns."

"That will be rather severe, won't it?" asked Ben.

"She deserves it; but I may do worse."

"How can that be?"

"Do you see that man over on the other side of the table—the short, red-haired man?"

"Yes, I see him."

"He is a chemist and has invented a compound a thousand times more powerful than dynamite. I am negotiating for it, and, if I succeed, I mean to blow the whole island out of the water. What do you think of that, eh?" he continued, triumphantly.

"I think in that case I shall keep away from England," answered Ben, keeping as straight a face as he could.

"Ah, you will do well."

When dinner was over, the boarders passed out of the room, Ben among them. He was destined not to go out quietly.

Suddenly a wild-looking woman darted toward him and threw her arms around his neck, exclaiming:

"At last I have found you, my son, my son !"

Ben struggled to release himself, assisted by Francois, who did not scruple to use considerable force.

"None of your tricks, madam !" he cried, angrily.

"Will you take from me my boy?" she exclaimed, piteously.

"There is some mistake. I am not your son," said Ben.

The woman shook her head sadly.

"He disowns his poor mother," she said, mournfully.

On the whole, Ben was rather glad to return to his chamber.

"I don't like my fellow-boarders," he thought. "I sha'n't stay in the *maison de fous* any longer than I am obliged to."

CHAPTER XXVII.

A MIDNIGHT ESCAPE.

FOR three days Ben passed a dull, uniform existence, being most of the time confined to his chamber. To a boy of active temperament it was most irksome. If he only had something to read, the hours would pass more swiftly. Fortunately, on the second day, he bethought himself of Francois, who seemed friendly.

"Francois," he said, "can't you get me something to read?"

"I don't know," said the attendant, doubtfully. "What would monsieur like?"

"Anything you can find. I would prefer a story."

"I will try, monsieur."

The next time Francois made his appearance he held in his hand a tattered edition of a popular novel.

" Will that do ?" he asked.

Ben had never heard of the book, but on opening its pages it looked attractive, and he answered :

" Yes, Francois, I am much obliged to you."

He thought it politic, remembering that he might need other favors, to put a franc piece into the hand of the friendly attendant.

Francois brightened up. His wages were so small that these little gratuities were very welcome.

" Would monsieur like something else ?" he inquired.

" There is one thing I would like very much, Francois," answered Ben.

" What is that, monsieur ?"

" To get out of this place."

" But monsieur is insane."

" I am no more insane than you are. Do I look insane ?"

" No; but one cannot always tell."

" I would give a hundred francs to any one who would get me out of this," said Ben, not, however, expecting to produce much impression on the mind of his auditor.

"A hundred francs!" repeated Francois, his eyes sparkling.

But in a moment he looked sober.

"It would not do. I should be discharged," he said.

"Think it over, Francois," said Ben.

The attendant did not answer, but the suggestion had borne fruit.

It may be asked how Ben had so much money. It may be explained that he was about to send a remittance home, having received a payment from Major Grafton, but his unexpected arrival at the refuge had prevented. He had with him two hundred francs, or about forty dollars in gold.

Something happened on the third day which worked favorably for Ben's hopes of securing the active assistance of Francois. About dusk a boy appeared at the gate of the asylum, and asked to see Francois.

When the two were brought together, he said:

"I came from your wife. She wishes you to come home. The child—little Marie—is very sick."

Poor Francois was much disturbed. In a little cottage five miles away lived his wife and his only child, Marie. The poor fellow was deeply attached to his child, for it must be remembered that the poor and simple-minded are quite as apt to have strong affections as the richer and more favored.

"Is she very bad, Jean?" he asked, quite pale.

"Yes," answered Jean. "I think she is out of her head. She keeps moaning. Her poor mother is very much frightened."

"I will ask if I can come," said Francois, and he straightway sought out the doctor.

"I would like to speak to you, M. Bourdon," he said.

"Speak quick, then, for I am busy," said the doctor, gruffly, for something had happened to disturb him.

"Jean Gault has just told me that my little Marie is very sick, and my wife wants me to come home. If I could go now, I would come back in the morning."

"Well, you can't go," said the doctor, harshly.

"But, *Monsieur le Docteur*, do you understand that my child—my little Marie—is very sick? She moans, and is out of her head, and I may never see her again, if I don't go."

"Plague take your little Marie!" said M. Bourdon, brutally. "What have I to do with her? I want you to stay here. You know very well that you can't be spared."

"But," protested Francois, indignantly, "do you think because I am poor that I have no feeling? You are very much mistaken. I cannot stay away and let poor Marie die without seeing her."

"You can't go, at all events," said M. Bourdon, roughly.

"I cannot go?"

"No; or, if you do, you will lose your place. I cannot have my men going away on every silly pretext. I don't believe your child is sick at all."

"But Jean Gault is below. He has brought word from my wife."

"I dare say it is all planned between you."

"Then you will not let me go?"

"No, I won't. If you go, you lose your

place. I shall not take you back. Do you understand?"

"Yes, I understand," said Francois, slowly.

"Then you can go. We have had words enough about this."

If the doctor had not been irritated he would have been careful how he dealt with Francois, who was the most valuable man in his employ. But when we are irritated we lose sight of what is politic, and are apt to make grievous mistakes, as M. Bourdon certainly did on this occasion.

Francois sought out little Jean.

"Jean," he said, "go home and tell my wife that I will come some time to-night. The doctor has forbidden me to go, but I shall go, all the same. Be sure you tell no one else."

"Very well, Francois," answered the boy.

"Tell my wife I may be late, but I will surely come."

The boy went away, and Francois went up to Ben's room.

"Monsieur, I have something to say to you," he commenced.

"What is it, Francois?"

16

"You said you would give a hundred francs to any one who would get you out of this?"

"Yes, Francois," answered Ben, quickly.

"Have you so much money with you, then?" asked Francois, doubtfully.

"See here!" and Ben took out five napoleons, which he displayed in his open palm.

The attendant's eyes sparkled.

"And you will give them to me, if perchance I set you free?"

"Yes."

"Listen, then. I would not do it, but my little Marie is very sick, and my wife wants me to come home. Perhaps she may die;" and the poor fellow suppressed a sob. "But M. Bordon—that is the doctor—he says I shall not go. He said 'Plague take your child!'" continued Francois, wrathfully.

"Poor Francois," said Ben compassionately.

"Ah! you feel for me, little monsieur," said Francois, gratefully. "The doctor has a heart like a stone. He says if I go I shall not come back; but I do not care, I cannot stay away. I will go, and you shall go with me. Can you walk five miles?"

"I can walk ten—fifteen, if necessary," said Ben, promptly.

"Then be ready at midnight. We will go together. It will not do to go earlier. Then the doctor will be asleep. Every one else will be asleep, and we can go away unobserved. M. Bourdon will be sorry that he did not let me go. I promised to come back." And Francois's eyes sparkled with honest indignation.

Ben's heart beat high with hope.

"You will come to my room at midnight?" he said.

"Yes, monsieur."

"I will be ready."

"One thing, monsieur. Do not have your shoes on. You can carry them in your hand. We must not make any noise when we are going down stairs, or we may be caught."

"That is well thought of, Francois. Depend upon me. I will be ready."

It will easily be supposed that Ben did not go to bed. He sat waiting patiently hour after hour till, as midnight struck, his door was softly opened, and Francois appeared.

"Now," said the attendant, "follow me, and make no noise."

Ben, in his stocking feet, followed the attendant down stairs. Producing a large key, Francois opened the outside door, then closed it softly, and they stood outside under a starlit sky.

CHAPTER XXVIII.

BEN'S FLIGHT.

AS good luck would have it, Ben and Francois departed without being observed. On emerging from the asylum they at first ran, after putting on their shoes, but when a quarter of a mile had been traversed they dropped into a walk.

"Well, we got away safely," said Ben.

"Yes; the doctor was asleep. We shall not be missed till morning."

"And then it shall be my fault if I am caught. Where is your home, Francois?"

"Five miles away."

"Yes, but is it on my way?"

"Where would monsieur go?"

"To Paris."

"To Paris!" ejaculated Francois, with wonderment. "That is a great way off, is it not?"

"Yes, I think it must be a thousand miles away."

"But monsieur is a boy; he cannot walk so far."

"No," answered Ben, laughing. "I don't propose to. Is there any railroad station near your house?"

"Yes, monsieur; only five minutes off."

"That will do very well."

"And has monsieur money enough?"

"Not to go all the way to Paris, but half-way there, perhaps."

"And is not monsieur afraid he will starve —without money?"

"I think I can get along," said Ben, slowly, for it dawned upon him that it would not be a very pleasant thing to be penniless in a foreign country.

"I will give back half the money monsieur has given me," said Francois, in a friendly tone.

"No, Francois; you will need it all. I am not afraid."

After a walk of an hour and a half the two pedestrians reached a small village set among the hills. Francois began to walk faster, and to look more eager.

"Does monsieur see that cottage?" he said.

Ben's eyes rested on an humble cottage just out of the village.

"Yes."

"It is mine. Will monsieur come with me?"

"Yes, I will go to see if your little girl is alive."

Soon they were at the door. There was a light burning in the main room. A plain, neat woman opened the door.

"Thank Heaven!" she exclaimed, "it is Francois."

"Is—is Marie alive?"

"Yes, my husband. She has had a change for the better."

"Heaven be praised!"

"And who is this young gentleman?"

"A friend," answered Francois, after some hesitation.

"Then I'm glad to see him. Welcome, monsieur."

"Come in, monsieur," said Francois.

"I think I had better go to the station."

"The cars will not start till seven o'clock. Monsieur will need repose."

"But I don't wish to incommode you."

"My wife will give you a blanket, and you can lie here."

Ben accepted the invitation, and stretched himself out on a settee.

"I will wake you in time," said Francois. "Be tranquil."

CHAPTER XXIX.

BEN IS MISSED.

MEANWHILE M. Bourdon slept the sleep of the just—or the unjust—not dreaming of the loss his establishment had sustained. He did not open his eyes till five o'clock.

Usually at that hour Francois was stirring, as he had morning duties to perform. But M. Bourdon did not hear him bustling around as usual. At first this did not strike him, but after awhile he began to wonder why.

"The lazy dog!" he said to himself. "He is indulging himself this morning, and his work will suffer."

He went to the door of his chamber and called "Francois!"

Francois slept in an upper room, but still the asylum was not a lofty building, and he should have heard.

"He must be fast asleep, as usual," grumbled M. Bourdon. "I must go up and rouse him. It would be well if I had a horsewhip."

Slipping on a part of his clothing, the doctor crept up stairs.

He knocked at the door of his dilatory servant.

"Francois! Francois, I say. Are you dead?"

There was no answer.

"I suppose he has locked his door," muttered the doctor, as he tried the latch.

But no! the door opened, and, to his dismay, the room was empty. The bed had not been disturbed.

The doctor's face was dark with anger.

"The ingrate has left me, after all. He has gone to his child, who is not sick at all, I dare say. Well, he will repent it. I will not take him back."

Here the doctor paused. It would be exceedingly inconvenient to lose Francois, who, besides being a capable man, accepted very small pay.

"At any rate I will lower his wages!" he

said. "He shall regret the way he has served me."

It was a temporary inconvenience. Still there was an outside man whom he could impress into the service as a substitute, and in a day or two Francois would be glad to return. It was not, perhaps, so serious a matter, after all.

But M. Bourdon changed his mind when he found the front door unlocked.

"Who had escaped, if any?"

This was the question he asked himself. In great haste he went from one room to another, but all seemed to be occupied. It was only when he opened Ben's room that he ascertained that the one whom he would most regret to lose had decamped. Ben's bed, too, was but little disturbed. He had slept on the outside, if he had slept at all, but not within the bed, as was but too evident.

"Has any one seen the boy?" demanded M. Bourdon of an outdoor servant who slept outside, but was already on duty.

"Not I, *Monsieur le Docteur*."

"Then he must have escaped with Francois! Put my horse in the carriage at once."

Ten minutes later M. Bourdon was on his way to the cottage of Francois.

Fifteen minutes before he arrived Francois had aroused our young hero.

"It is time to get up, little monsieur," he said. "In half an hour the cars will start."

Refreshed by his sound sleep, Ben sprang up at once—he did not need to dress—and was ready for the adventures of the day.

"Where is the station, Francois?" he said.

"I will go with monsieur."

"No; if the doctor should come, delay him so that he cannot overtake me."

"Perhaps it is best."

Ben followed the directions of his humble friend, and soon brought up at the station. He purchased a third-class ticket for a place fifty miles away, and waited till it was time for the train to start.

Meanwhile M. Bourdon had driven up to the cottage of Francois.

The door was opened to him by Francois himself.

"Where is that boy?" Did he come away with you?" he asked, abruptly.

"What boy?" asked Francois, vacantly.

"The one who came a few days since. You know who I mean."

Francois shrugged his shoulders.

"Is he gone?" he asked.

"Of course he is, fool."

Just then the wife of Francois came to the door. Unfortunately her husband had not warned her, nor did she know that Ben had been an inmate of the asylum.

"Where is the boy who came here last night with your husband?" asked M. Bourdon, abruptly.

"Gone to the station," answered the woman, unsuspiciously.

The doctor jumped into his carriage, and drove with speed to the station.

CHAPTER XXX.

M. BOURDON'S LITTLE SCHEME.

MEANWHILE Ben had entered a third-class carriage—it behooved him to be economical now—and sat down. He was congratulating himself on his fortunate escape, when M. Bourdon dashed up to the station.

He entered the building, and was about passing to the platform, when he was stopped.

"Your ticket, monsieur."

Just then came the signal for the train to start.

"Never mind the ticket!" shouted the doctor. "Don't stop me. One of my patients is running away."

"I can't help it," said the guard, imperturbably. "Monsieur cannot pass without a ticket."

"But I don't want to go anywhere," roared M. Bourdon. "I want to see the passengers."

To the railway attendant this seemed a very

curious request.   He began to think the doctor, with his excitable manner, was insane.
At any rate, he was obliged to obey the rules.

"Go back and buy a ticket, monsieur," he
said, unmoved.

"But I don't want to go anywhere," protested M. Bourdin.

"Then go back!" And the official, placing
his hand on the doctor's sacred person, thrust
him forcibly aside.

"Fool! Dolt!" screamed M. Bourdon,
who could hear the train starting.

"You must be crazy!" said the guard,
shrugging his shoulders.

It was too late now.   The train had actually
gone, and M. Bourdon turned back, foiled,
humiliated and wrathful.   He regretted bit-
terly now that he had not let Francois off the
evening before, as in that case Ben would not
have had a chance to escape.   Now he must
lose the generous sum which Major Grafton
had agreed to pay for his ward.   It was more
than he received for any other of his patients,
for M. Bourdon, recognizing Ben's sanity,
shrewdly surmised that the guardian had

some special design in having his ward locked up, and took advantage of it to increase the weekly sum which he charged.

And now all this was lost.

But no! A happy thought struck the worthy doctor. Ben had escaped, it is true, but why could not he go on charging for him just as before? His escape was not known to Major Grafton, and probably would not be discovered for a long time at least. The major was not very likely to visit the asylum, as an interview between him and his young victim would be rather embarrassing to him.

Yes, that was the course he would pursue. He would from time to time send in a report of his patient, and regularly collect his board, while he would be at no expense whatever for him. It was necessary, however, to take Francois into his confidence, and he drove back to the cottage of the humble attendant.

Francois was watching outside. He was afraid the doctor would succeed in capturing the boy, in whom he had begun to feel a strong interest. When he saw M. Bourdon

drive up alone he smiled to himself, though
his features remained outwardly grave.

"Did you find him, sir?" he asked, respectfully.

"No," answered M. Bourdon, roughly.
"The train had just started."

"And was he a passenger?"

"Doubtless."

"What will you do, *Monsieur le Docteur?*"
Francois asked, curiously.

"Francois," said M. Bourdon, suddenly,
"I am sorry for you."

"Why?" asked Francois, considerably surprised. "Is it because my little Marie is
sick?"

"Plague take your little Marie! It is because you have helped the boy to escape."

"How could I help him, sir?"

"Some one must have unlocked the door
of his room. Otherwise, he could not have
got out."

"I don't know, monsieur," said Francois,
assuming ignorance.

"When did you first see him?"

"I had walked about a quarter of a mile,"

17

said Francois, mendaciously, "when he ran up and overtook me. I told him to go back, but he would not. He followed me, and came here."

"This story is by no means ingenious," said the doctor, shaking his head. "When you stand up in a court of justice you will see how the lawyers will make you eat your words. And very likely they will send you to prison."

"Oh, no! Don't say that!" said poor Francois, much frightened. "What would become of my poor wife and child?"

"You should have thought of them before this."

"Oh, *Monsieur le Docteur*, you will save me from prison!" exclaimed poor, simple-minded Francois.

"On one condition."

"Name it, monsieur."

"Let no one know that the boy has escaped."

"I will not, if you desire it."

"You see, it will be bad for me as well as for you. It was very important to keep him

—very important, indeed—and his friends will call me to account. But they need not know it, if you remain silent."

"No one shall hear me say a word, *Monsieur le Docteur,*" said Francois, promptly.

"That is well. In that case I will overlook your disobedience, and allow you to return to your place."

"Oh, monsieur is too good!" said Francois, who did not by any means anticipate such magnanimous forgiveness.

"When can you come back?"

"When monsieur will."

"Come, then, this evening. It will be in time. I will allow you to spend the day with your family, since your child is sick."

The doctor turned his horse's head, and drove back to the asylum.

Three days after he wrote to Major Grafton:

"My DEAR SIR: Your ward is rather sullen, but quiet. He was at first disposed to make trouble, but the firm and effective discipline of the institution has had the usual result. I allow him to amuse himself with reading, as this seems to be the best way of keeping him quiet and contented. His insanity is of a mild kind, but it is often precisely such cases that are most difficult to cure. You may rely, Monsieur Grafton, upon my taking the best care of the young gentleman, and, as you desired, I will especially guard against his obtaining writing materials, lest, by a misrepresentation of his condition, he might excite his friends.

"I thank you for your promptness in forwarding my weekly payments. Write me at any time when you desire a detailed account of your ward's condition."

M. Bourdon signed this letter, after reading it over to himself, with a complacent smile. He reflected that it did great credit to his ingenuity.

"Some men would have revealed the truth," he said to himself, "and lost a fine income. I am wiser."

In due time this letter reached Major Grafton.

"That is well," he said to himself. "I am rather sorry for the boy, but he has brought it on himself. Why must he be a fool, and threaten to blab? He was living in luxury, such as he has never been accustomed to before, and he might rest content with that. In me surely he had an indulgent master. I rarely gave him anything to do. He could live on the fat of the land, see the world at no expense to himself, and have all the advantages of a rich man's son. Well, he has made his own bed, and now he must lie in it. On some accounts it is more agreeable to me to travel alone, and have no one to bother me."

To avert suspicion, Major Grafton left the Hotel des Bergues and took up his quarters at another hotel. At the end of two weeks he left for Italy, having arranged matters satisfactorily by sending M. Bourdon a month's payment in advance, an arrangement that suited the worthy doctor remarkably well.

CHAPTER XXXI.

A WANDERER IN FRANCE.

A BOY toiled painfully over a country road but a few miles from the city of Lyons. His clothes bore the marks of the dusty road over which he was travelling. It was clear by his appearance that he was not a French boy. There is no need of keeping up a mystery which my young readers will easily penetrate. This boy was our hero, Ben Baker. He was now more than half way to Paris, and might have reached that gay city days since but for his limited supply of money. When he gave Francois a hundred francs he nearly exhausted his limited capital, but there was no help for it.

He had travelled a hundred miles on the railway, far enough to be beyond the danger of pursuit and the risk of a return to the asylum, which he could not think of without a shudder. Now he would walk, and so economize. He had walked another hundred miles, and had reached this point in his journey. But his scanty funds were now reduced to a piece of two sous, and he was between three and four thousand miles from home. This very day he had walked fifteen miles, and all he had eaten was a roll, which he had purchased in a baker's shop in a country village through which he had passed in the early morning.

Hopeful as Ben was by temperament, he looked sober enough as he contemplated his position. How was he ever to return home, and what prospect was there for him in Europe? If he had been in any part of America he would have managed to find something to do, but here he felt quite helpless.

He had walked fifteen miles on an almost empty stomach, and the result was that he was not only tired but sleepy. He sat down by the way-side, with his back against the trunk of a tree, and before he was conscious of it he had fallen asleep.

How long he had been asleep he did not

know, but he was roused suddenly by a touch.
Opening his eyes, he saw a man fumbling at
his watch-chain. The man, who was a stout
and unprepossessing-looking man of about
thirty-five, wearing a blouse, jumped back
with a hasty, confused exclamation.

"What are you doing?" demanded Ben,
suspiciously.

He spoke first in English, but, remembering
himself, repeated the question in French.

"Pardon, monsieur," said the man, looking
uncomfortable.

Ben's glance fell on his chain and the
watch, which had slipped from his pocket,
and he understood that the man had been trying to steal his watch. In spite of his poverty
and need of money he had not yet parted
with the watch, though he suspected the time
would soon come when he should be compelled to do so.

"You were trying to steal my watch," said
Ben, severely.

"No, monsieur, you are wrong," answered
the tramp, for that was what he would be
called in America.

"How came my watch out of the pocket, and why were you leaning over me?" continued Ben.

"I wanted to see what time it was," answered the man, after a minute's hesitation.

"I think it is fortunate I awoke when I did," said Ben.

His new acquaintance did not choose to notice the significance of the words.

"Monsieur," he said," "I am a poor man. Will you help me with a few sous?"

Ben could not help laughing. It seemed too ridiculous that any one should ask money of him. He took the two-sous piece from his pocket.

"Do you see that?" he asked.

"Yes, monsieur."

"It is all the money I have."

The man looked incredulous.

"And yet monsieur is well dressed, and has a gold watch."

"Still I am as poor as you, for I am more than three thousand miles from home, and have not money enough to get there, even if I sell my watch."

"Where does monsieur live?" asked the tramp, looking interested.

"In America."

"Will monsieur take my advice?"

"If it is good."

"There is a rich American gentleman at the Hotel de la Couronne, in Lyons. He would, perhaps, help monsieur."

The idea struck Ben favorably. This gentleman could, at any rate, give him advice, and he felt that he needed it.

"How far is Lyons away?"

"Scarcely a league."

"Straight ahead?"

"Yes, monsieur."

"Then I will go there."

"And I, too. I will guide monsieur."

"Thank you. I will reward you, if I have the means."

CHAPTER XXXII.

A STRANGE MEETING.

THE Hotel de la Couronne is situated in one of the finest parts of Lyons. As Ben stood before it, he began to doubt whether he had not better go away with his errand undone. After all, this American gentleman, if there were one in the hotel, would be likely to feel very little interest in a destitute boy claiming to be a fellow-countryman. He might even look upon him as a designing rogue, with a fictitious story of misfortune, practising upon his credulity. Ben's cheek flushed at the mere thought that he might be so regarded.

So he was on the point of going away; but he was nerved by his very desperation to carry out his original plan.

He entered the hotel, and went up to the office.

" Will monsieur look at some apartments ?" asked the landlord's son, a man of thirty.

" No, monsieur—that is, not at present. Is there an American gentleman at present staying in the hotel ?"

" Yes. Is monsieur an American ?"

Ben replied in the affirmative, and asked for the name of his countryman.

" It is Monsieur Novarro," was the reply.

"Novarro!" repeated Ben to himself. "That sounds more like a Spanish or an Italian name."

" Is that the gentleman monsieur desires to see ?"

"From what part of America does Mr. Novarro come?"

The register was applied to, and the answer given was " Havana."

"Havana!" said Ben, disappointed. "Then he will take no interest in me," he thought. "There is very little kindred between a Cuban and an American."

"Would monsieur like to see M. Novarro?"

"I may as well see him," thought Ben, and he answered in the affirmative.

"There is M. Novarro, now," said the land-lord's son ; and Ben, turning, saw a tall, very dark-complexioned man, who had just entered.

"M. Novarro, here is a young gentleman who wishes to see you—a countryman of yours."

The Cuban regarded Ben attentively, and not without surprise.

"Have we met before?" he asked, courteously.

"No, sir," answered Ben, relieved to find that the Cuban spoke English ; "and I am afraid I am taking a liberty in asking for you."

"By no means! If I can be of any service to you, my friend, you may command me."

"It is rather a long story, Mr. Novarro," Ben commenced.

"Then we will adjourn to my room, where we shall be more at our ease."

Ben followed his new acquaintance to a handsome private parlor on the second floor and seated himself in a comfortable arm-chair, indicated by the Cuban.

"I will first mention my name," said Ben. "It is Benjamin Baker."

"Baker!" exclaimed the Cuban, in evident excitement. "Who was your father?"

"My father was Dr. John Baker, and lived in Sunderland, Connecticut."

"Is is possible!" ejaculated the Cuban; "you are his son?"

"Did you know my father?" asked Ben, in amazement.

"I never saw him, but I knew of him. I am prepared to be a friend to his son. Now tell me your story."

CHAPTER XXXIII.

AN ASTOUNDING DISCOVERY.

BEN told his story so far as it concerned his engagement by Major Grafton and his visit to Europe. Of his mother and her circumstances and of his uncle he had scarcely occasion to speak, considering that his auditor would hardly feel interested in his own personal history. The Cuban, who had a grave, kindly aspect, listened with close attention to his narrative. When Ben ceased speaking he said:

"My young friend, there is one thing that puzzles me in this story of yours."

"What is it, sir?" asked Ben, anxiously. He feared that the stranger did not believe him.

"Why should you need to travel with Major Grafton, or any other gentleman, as private secretary, unless, indeed, your mother did not wish you to come to Europe alone?"

Ben stared at his interlocutor in amazement.

"How could I come to Europe alone?" he asked. "Where should I find the money to pay my expenses?"

"Your mother might pay the expenses of your trip."

"My mother is very poor, Mr. Novarro."

"Very poor! Has she, then, lost the money that your father left her?"

"I think you must be under a great mistake, Mr. Novarro. My uncle allows my mother a small income, and I help her all I can."

"There is certainly a great mistake somewhere," said the Cuban. "To my certain knowledge your father possessed a hundred thousand dollars in first-class securities. Didn't you know anything of this?" continued Mr. Novarro, observing Ben's look of extreme amazement.

"I know nothing of it, Mr. Novarro."

"Then he must have been robbed of the securities which I myself gave him on the 18th day of May, in the year 18—"

"That was the day of my father's death," said Ben.

"He died on that very day?" said the Cuban in excitement. "Tell me the particulars of your father's death. Did he die a natural death?"

"Yes, sir; he died of heart disease."

"And where?"

"In the house of my Uncle Nicholas."

"Before he had time to go home? Before he had acquainted your mother with his good fortune?"

"Neither my mother nor myself knew but that he died a poor man."

"But he had the securities with him. Did your uncle say nothing of them?"

"Not a word."

A look of suspicion appeared on the face of Filippo Novarro.

"Tell me," he said, quickly—"did your uncle, shortly after your father's death, enlarge his business?"

"Yes, sir; he moved from a small store in Grand street to a larger store on Broadway— the one which he now occupies."

18

With the Cuban, suspicion was now changed to certainty.

He brought down his fist heavily upon the table at his side.

"I know all now," he said. "Your uncle deliberately robbed your dead father of the securities which I had placed in his hands, and coolly appropriating them to his own use, used the proceeds to build up and extend his business, leaving your mother to live in poverty."

"I feel bewildered," said Ben. "I can hardly believe my uncle would treat us so shamefully."

"By the way, when did your mother move to Minnesota?" asked the Cuban.

"To Minnesota?"

"Yes. When I was in New York, not long since, I called upon your uncle and signified my intention to call upon your mother. He told me she had moved to Minnesota, and, of course, I was compelled to give up my plan."

"My mother has never moved to Minnesota; she still lives in Sunderland."

"Then your uncle intended to prevent our meeting. He feared, doubtless, that if we met, his rascality would be discovered. Providence has defeated his cunningly-devised scheme, and the truth will soon be brought to light, to his confusion."

"I am afraid, sir, it will be difficult for my mother and myself to prove that my father left money. We have no money with which to hire legal assistance."

"I propose to take the matter into my own hands. I am personally interested as the agent whom my dead friend commissioned to pay a debt of gratitude to the man who saved his life. Have you anything to detain you in Europe?"

"No, sir, except an empty purse."

"Permit me to act as your banker."

Mr. Novarro drew from his pocket two hundred and fifty francs in gold and paper and handed them to Ben.

To our hero it seemed like a fairy-tale, in which he was playing the leading part. He half-feared that the gold would turn into brass and the bank-notes into withered leaves; but,

strange though it was, he saw good reason to
think that his good fortune was real.

"How can I thank you, sir, for your liberality?" he said, gratefully.

"You forget that this is your own money;
I am only advancing it to you, and shall be
repaid speedily. Will you accept me as your
guardian to protect your interests and com-
pel your uncle to disgorge his ill-gotten
gains?"

"Thankfully, sir, if you are willing to take
the trouble."

"Then you will sail with me for New York
by the next steamer. Have you your luggage
with you?"

"I have nothing, sir, except what I have on
my back. I had to leave the asylum without
a change, and I have not been able to change
my clothes for a week or more."

"I had forgotten. This must be looked to
at once. We will take lunch, and then go
out and purchase a new supply of under-
clothing."

Once more Ben had fallen on his feet. At
what appeared to be the darkest moment light

had suddenly fallen across his path, and he had stumbled upon the one man who was able to bring him into the sunshine. Before night his wardrobe had been quite replenished, and he breathed a deep sigh of relief as he found himself in fresh and clean attire.

He sought out the tramp who had escorted him to the hotel, and liberally rewarded him.

"I shall telegraph for passage in the Havre line of steamships," said Mr. Novarro. "A steamer is to sail on Saturday, so that we shall not have long to wait."

"I fear, Mr. Novarro, you are interrupting your own plans in order to befriend me," said Ben to his new patron.

"I have no plans. I am—perhaps unfortunately for myself—a rich man, under no necessity of labor. Indeed, my chief aim has been to pass my time as pleasantly as possible. Now I find something to do, and I find myself happier for having some object in life. I am rejoiced that we have met. It has brought to my life a new interest; and even after I have redeemed your wrongs I shall hope to keep up my acquaintance with you, and to make the acquaintance of your mother."

"You may be sure, sir, that my mother will be only too glad to know so true a friend."

The Cuban regarded Ben with a look of interest and affection. He was beginning to be attracted to him for his own sake. He was a man of energetic temperament, though a large inheritance had hitherto prevented any display of energy. At length the occasion had arisen, and he looked forward with eagerness to the struggle with the New York merchant to secure the rights of his new friend.

On the next day Ben and his guardian left Lyons for Paris. They had two days in this lovely city, and late on Friday evening they reached Havre, the point where they were to embark for America.

"The first act is over, Ben," said the Cuban. "Our ocean trip is a long wait between the first and second acts. When the curtain next rises it will be in New York, and there will be other actors to take an unwilling part in our drama, which is devoted to the detection and punishment of guilt."

CHAPTER XX.XIV.

ROSE MAKES AN ENEMY.

LEAVING Ben and his new guardian on their passage across the Atlantic, we will precede them to New York, and inquire after the welfare of some of our other characters.

The Beauforts seemed to have entered on a new and prosperous career. Rose continued to give lessons in music, and to receive liberal compensation. She was really an accomplished musician, and had the happy knack of making herself agreeable to her young pupils. Besides, she was backed by the influence of Miss Wilmot, and that helped her not a little. Her sister Adeline, too, gave lessons in art, and thus contributed to the family purse.

My readers will not have forgotten the young man who rescued Rose from the disagreeable attentions of her elderly lover, Mr. Parkinson. More than once Rose had thought

of Clinton Randall, and, though she scarcely
admitted it to herself, cherished the hope that
they would some day meet again. The young
man's frank, chivalrous manners, and handsome face and figure, had impressed her most
favorably, and she suffered herself to think
of him more than she would have liked to
admit. Had she known that Clinton Randall
had been equally attracted by her, and had
made strenuous efforts to find her ever since
their first meeting, she would have been much
gratified.

Some weeks passed, however, before she
saw him again. One afternoon, as she was
walking through Madison Square on her way
home from Mrs. Tilton's, where she had given
her customary lessons, she met the young man
in the walk.

His face glowed with unmistakable joy as
he hurried forward, with hand extended.

"I am very glad to meet you again, Miss
Beaufort," he said, eagerly. "Where have
you been? Not out of the city?"

"Oh, no!" answered Rose, successfully concealing her own pleasure at the meeting.

"You can't expect a poor music-teacher to break away from her work at this season?"

"But I did not know you were a music-teacher."

"No, I suppose not," answered Rose, smiling.

"Do you give lessons on the piano?"

"Yes, it is my only instrument."

"I have for a long time thought of taking lessons on the piano," said Randall, who had never thought of it before, "if I could only find a teacher who would not be too strict. Do you—take gentlemen?"

"I am afraid I could not venture upon a pupil of your age, Mr. Randall," said Rose, amused. "Suppose you proved refractory?"

"But I never would."

"I am afraid my time is fully occupied. I will promise, however, to take you, if I agree to take any gentlemen."

"Thank you. I shall not forget your promise."

Clinton Randall, though he had been walking in a different direction, turned and accompanied Rose, both chatting easily and familiarly. It never occurred to Rose that she might meet any one who would comment upon her and her escort. But at the corner of Eighteenth street and Broadway she met a tall young lady, who made her the slightest possible nod, while she fixed eyes of scorn and displeasure upon the two. Clinton Randall raised his hat, and they parted.

"You know Miss Jayne, then, Miss Beaufort," said Randall.

"Yes, slightly, and you?"

"I have met her in society."

"She is a niece of Mrs. Tilton, to whose daughters I am giving music-lessons."

"Indeed! I know Mrs. Tilton—I am to attend her party next week. Shall you be there?"

"I believe so—not as a guest, however. She has invited me to play on the piano for the entertainment of the guests. You will probably dance to my music."

"I would rather dance with you to the music of another player, Miss Beaufort."

"You forget, Mr. Randall, that I am a poor music-teacher."

"I don't think of it at all. It makes no difference in your claims to consideration."

"The world does not agree with you, Mr. Randall."

"Then it ought. By the way, Miss Beaufort, has your elderly admirer renewed his proposals?"

"Mr. Parkinson? No, I have not met him since."

"You are sure you won't relent, and make him a happy man?"

"I don't think it at all likely," said Rose, laughing.

Meanwhile Rose had made an enemy without being aware of it.

Miss Arethusa Jayne had long looked upon Clinton Randall with eyes of partiality, not alone on account of his good looks, but because he was wealthy, socially distinguished, and in all respects a desirable *parti*. In her vanity she had thought that he was not indifferent to her attractions. When, therefore, she saw him walking with her aunt's music-teacher, she was not only angry but jealous. She reluctantly admitted that Rose was pretty,

though she considered herself still more so.
After this meeting she changed her plans, and
went straight to her aunt.

"Aunt," she said, "whom do you think I
met on Broadway just now?"

"I am sure I can't tell, Arethusa. I suppose all the world and his wife are out this
fine day."

"Your music-teacher, Miss Beaufort, and
Clinton Randall."

"You don't say so!" ejaculated Mrs. Tilton.
"How should she know him?"

"I have no idea they were ever introduced,"
said Arethusa, sneering. "Probably she isn't
particular how she makes acquaintance with
gentlemen. I always thought her forward."

"I can't say I ever did, Arethusa."

"Oh, she covers it up with you; but I ask
you, Aunt Lucy, how could she otherwise get
acquainted with a gentleman of Mr. Randall's
position?"

"I don't know. Was she actually walking
with him?"

"Certainly, and laughing and talking in a
boisterous, unladylike way."

Of course this was untrue, but a jealous woman is not likely to consider her words.

"I thought you ought to know it, aunt, so I came and told you."

"Do you think I ought to do anything, Arethusa?"

"I would not allow such a girl to teach my children."

"But she is an excellent teacher, and is recommended by Miss Wilmot."

"Probably Miss Wilmot does not know how she conducts herself. No doubt she carefully conceals her forwardness from that lady."

"But I can't discharge her without giving reasons."

"True, aunt. By the way, Mr. Randall comes to your party, does he not?"

"He has sent an acceptance."

"And you mean to have Miss Beaufort there to play dancing-tunes?"

"Yes; she comes a good deal cheaper than a professional," said Mrs. Tilton, who, even in her pleasures, was thrifty.

"That is well. Then you will have an opportunity to see how the two go on together, and can quietly signify to Miss Beaufort, the next day, your opinion of her conduct."

"But, Arethusa," said Mrs. Tilton, who was not jealous, like her niece, "I can't think there is anything out of the way. Miss Beaufort has always seemed to me a model of propriety."

"Oh, you dear, unsuspicious aunt! How easily you are deceived! Do you want to know my opinion of Miss Propriety—the opinion I formed when I first saw her?"

"Well, Arethusa?"

"I saw at once that she was bold and sly, and I really think it is taking a great risk to permit your children to be under the instruction of such a girl."

"Well, Arethusa, I will take your advice and watch them both at the party."

"That is all I ask, Aunt Lucy."

"I will get aunt to discharge her yet," said Miss Jayne to herself, with satisfied malice.

CHAPTER XXXV.

A WOMAN'S JEALOUSY.

M RS. TILTON'S house was ablaze with light, for it was the evening of the great party. Ambitious of social distinction, she took care to do things on a handsome scale, though she was not averse to saving money where it would not attract attention.

Among the young ladies present were two with whom we are especially concerned. One of them was Arethusa Jayne, who was dressed with more splendor than taste. She made a profuse display of jewelry, some of which, we may confidentially inform the reader, was borrowed from a well-known jeweler, who was handsomely paid for the favor. Of course no one suspected this, and the society young men were misled into thinking that the owner of so many diamonds must be very rich. This was precisely what Arethusa desired, for she was in the market, and had been for more years than she liked to remember.

Another young lady, still better known to us, was Rose Beaufort. She was the most plainly dressed young lady in the handsome parlors, yet she attracted an unusual share of attention.

"Who is that pretty young lady?" asked a middle-aged lady of Arethusa.

"That?" answered Miss Jayne, with a sneer. "Oh, that is Miss Beaufort, the music-teacher."

"She is very sweet-looking."

"Do you think so? I don't at all agree with you. To me she looks very artful, and I have reason to think that beneath her innocent exterior there is something quite different."

"That is a pity."

"It is not surprising. Still water runs deep, you know."

Rose kept in the background. She had no wish to make herself conspicuous at Mrs. Tilton's gay party. She would rather not have been there, but did not wish to disappoint her employer.

"Ah, here you are, Miss Beaufort," said a glad voice.

Rose looked up, and her face flushed with pleasure as she recognized Clinton Randall.

"I did not think you would find me," she said.

"I was sure to do it. I have been looking for you everywhere. Can't you spare a seat for me?"

Rose moved, and Clinton sat down beside her on the sofa. He had scarcely been there two minutes, however, when Arethusa discovered them. She went straightway to her aunt.

"Aunt Lucy," she said, in a low voice, "look at the sofa opposite."

"Well?" said Mrs. Tilton, who was rather short-sighted.

"There is your precious music-teacher monopolizing Clinton Randall. Didn't I tell you?"

"I am really shocked at her brazen ways. You were right, Arethusa."

"For goodness' sake, separate them before the whole room notices them."

19

"How can I do it?"

"Send her to the piano."

"Miss Beaufort," said Mrs. Tilton, coldly, "oblige me by sitting down to the piano. You may play a waltz."

"Certainly, Mrs. Tilton," said Rose.

"That woman speaks as if she owned Miss Beaufort," thought young Randall.

He was about to follow her to the piano when Arethusa came up, and with an insinuating smile, said:

"Don't look so mournful, Mr. Randall. Let me fill Miss Beaufort's place."

"Certainly," answered the young man, moving, but not with alacrity.

"I wasn't aware that you knew Miss Beaufort," said the young lady.

"I believe you saw me walking with her the other day."

"Yes, to be sure; it had escaped my mind."

Rose began to play. Her touch was fine, and her performance could hardly fail to attract attention.

"Miss Beaufort plays remarkably well," said Clinton Randall.

"Oh, it's her business," answered Arethusa, with careless hauteur. "She gives lessons to my aunt's children, you know."

"Your aunt is fortunate to secure such an accomplished pianist."

"Oh, she is very well," said Arethusa, carelessly. "Do you feel like dancing?"

"I beg your pardon. I should have suggested it."

The two moved out upon the floor and took their places among the dancers. Arethusa danced passably, her partner remarkably well. At length he led her to her seat, and, with a bow, left her, much to her chagrin.

Later in the evening some one relieved Rose at the piano. Clinton took the earliest opportunity to seek her out and ask her for a dance.

Rose hesitated.

"I have not danced for a long time," she said. "Circumstances have kept me out of society. I am afraid you won't find me a satisfactory partner."

"I will take the risk, Miss Beaufort. You won't refuse?"

She rose and took her place on the floor. Arethusa Jayne, who was dancing with one of the walking gentlemen of society, a young man who was merely invited to swell the number of guests, was not long in discovering Miss Beaufort's good luck, and her face showed her displeasure. It would have pleased her had Rose been awkward, but she was unusually graceful, in spite of her want of practice. Miss Jayne was hot with jealousy.

"You shall repent this," she said to herself, and looked so stern that her partner asked, with alarm:

"Are you not well, Miss Jayne?"

"Certainly"—you fool! she would liked to have added. "Why do you ask?"

"I thought you looked disturbed," he stammered.

"I was only a little thoughtful," she said, with a constrained smile. "But I am fatigued. Suppose we sit down."

He led her to her seat, nothing loth, and she had the satisfaction of following with her glance Clinton Randall and her rival five minutes more.

"Did you have a good time, Rose?" asked her sister Adeline, next morning, at the break-fast-table.

"Better than I dared to hope," answered Rose, with a smile.

"Did you dance?"

"Two or three times."

She had danced with two partners besides Clinton Randall, and with him a second time.

"It seemed quite like the old times," she said, after a pause, "when we were in society. Though I only appeared in the character of a governess, I enjoyed it."

"Don't you feel tired?"

"A little; but I don't go out to give lessons till afternoon."

At two o'clock Rose went to Mrs. Tilton's to give her regular lessons.

"Mrs. Tilton would like to see you," said the servant.

A little surprised, Rose remained in the parlor till that lady appeared.

"I wish to speak to you, Miss Beaufort," said Mrs. Tilton, coldly, "about your conduct last evening."

"My conduct last evening!" repeated Rose, in utter surprise. "To what do you refer?"

"To your indelicate conduct with Mr. Clinton Randall and other gentlemen."

"What do you mean? I demand an explanation!" exclaimed Rose, indignantly.

"You seem to forget your position, Miss Beaufort. As the instructress of my children, I feel I must be exacting. I do not approve of your bold flirtation with gentlemen above yourself in social position, and I beg to say that I must provide myself with another music-teacher for my girls."

"After your insulting remarks," said Rose, hotly, "nothing would induce me to remain in charge of them. Nothing in my conduct has called for such cruel charges."

"Doubtless you think so. I disagree with you," said Mrs. Tilton, coldly.

"Good-afternoon, madam!" said Rose, rising abruptly.

"Good-afternoon, Miss Beaufort."

It was like a thunderbolt to Rose, and mystified as well as made her indignant. She could recall nothing that had passed which

would justify Mrs. Tilton in her strange treatment.

It was the first blow, but not the last. Arethusa Jayne, with unappeased malice, went
the rounds of the families in which Rose was
employed, and within a week she received
notes from all the parents, expressing regret
that they could no longer avail themselves of
her services.

It began to look serious for poor Rose.

CHAPTER XXXVI.

ROSE COMES INTO A FORTUNE.

BEN and his friend had a fair passage from Liverpool, and were equally pleased to set foot on American soil. By this time they had become excellent friends. The Cuban, having no near relatives, was surprised to find how much interest he felt in his young ward.

"Well, Ben," he said, "shall we first attend to your business, or that of the young ladies whom your late employer has cheated out of their rightful inheritance?"

"My business can wait, Mr. Novarro. Let us attend to the last."

"Do you remember the office of Mr. Codicil—that was the name of the trustee, was it not?"

"Yes, sir. I can guide you there without delay."

"Then, after we are fairly established in our hotel, we will go to see him."

Meanwhile there was great despondency in the modest home of the Beauforts. To be deprived of her pupils without just cause was indeed a grievous misfortune, and, gentle as she was, Rose could not think of it without exasperation. Though she could not at first understand from whom the blow came, reflection satisfied her that Miss Arethusa Jayne was her enemy and had wrought this mischief. Her motive Rose could not penetrate, not being in the secret of Miss Jayne's admiration for Mr. Randall. To make matters worse, her constant friend, Miss Wilmot, was absent from the city, at some springs in Virginia, and was not expected home for some weeks to come. She applied for a position in answer to an advertisement, but when called upon for references her heart sank within her, as she reflected that the ladies who had recently employed her would hardly speak in her favor.

"What shall we do, Addie?" she asked, despondently. "I can't get new pupils, and I must do something. I don't like to go back to the old business of making vests."

"Don't do that, at any rate, Rose; I am sure you can do better than that."

"I wish I knew what."

"Suppose you go and see Mr. Codicil."

"He might think I wished him to give me money."

"No; ask him to use his influence to obtain you music-pupils."

Rose brightened at the suggestion.

"I believe I will follow your advice, Addie. It seems to me good."

"And if that doesn't do any good, write to Miss Wilmot, and ask her advice. You can always refer to her."

"Why, Addie, I never gave you credit for such wise counsel. Your words have inspired me with new cheerfulness. I will go to Mr. Codicil to-morrow morning."

Half an hour before the arrival of Rose Beaufort at the lawyer's office, Ben and Mr. Novarro entered.

"Can I see Mr. Codicil?" asked Ben.

The clerk said, doubtfully, noting Ben's youthful appearance, and judging that his business could not be of great importance:

"I will see. What name shall I mention?"

"You may say that I come from Major Grafton."

This message brought an immediate invitation to enter the lawyer's sanctum.

The old man regarded him with considerable surprise as he entered.

"I thought you were in Europe, Philip," he said. "Is your guardian with you?"

"I have just come from Europe, Mr. Codicil," answered Ben. "Major Grafton is not with me."

"How does it happen that you have left him? You have not run away, have you?"

"Yes, sir; I felt obliged to run away."

"May I ask why?" demanded the lawyer, searchingly.

"Because I was not willing to aid Major Grafton in a scheme of fraud."

Mr. Codicil pricked up his ears.

"Proceed, young man," he said. "This is becoming interesting."

"You called me Philip Grafton, and this is the name Major Grafton wished me to assume, but it is not my real name."

"Go on, go on!"

"My real name is Ben Baker. Major Grafton met me in this city, and engaged me to travel with him as his private secretary. He gave me the name of Philip Grafton, because, he said, I looked like his only son, bearing that name, who died abroad."

"The old rascal!"

"I supposed this was true, and saw no objection to the plan."

"Can you tell me what became of the boy whose name you assumed?" asked Mr. Codicil, eagerly.

"Yes, sir; he is dead."

"Poor fellow! Where did he die?"

"In Italy, last year."

"And his rascally guardian, concealing this from me, has drawn the income of his property regularly for his own use. Now tell me how you came to learn all this."

Ben gave the explanation clearly, and recited the steps taken by Major Grafton to keep him from divulging the secret.

"It was a bold game," said the lawyer; "but, thanks to your information, it has failed.

I shall at once telegraph to Major Grafton that his guardianship has ceased, and I will send over an agent to obtain the necessary proof of the boy's death."

At this moment a clerk entered.

"There is a young lady who desires to see you, Mr. Codicil."

"Did she give her name?"

"Miss Beaufort."

"Send her in at once. She could not have come at a more fitting time. My young friend, go into the little room adjoining, and wait till I summon you."

Rose Beaufort entered the lawyer's presence with a grave expression on her face.

"I hope, Mr. Codicil, you will excuse my troubling you with a visit."

"So far from troubling me, I am very glad to see you. What can I do for you?"

"I am in trouble, and wish your advice."

"Proceed."

Rose unfolded her story, and concluded by asking Mr. Codicil if he would exert his influence toward obtaining her some pupils in music.

The lawyer's eyes twinkled behind his spectacles.

"I hardly know what to say to that request," he answered.

"I did not suppose you would be prejudiced against me by Mrs. Tilton's false and groundless accusations," said Rose, with a troubled air.

"I am not. That is not the point. I am only questioning the expediency of your teaching at all."

"But I know of no better way of earning a livelihood."

"Still, it is not customary for wealthy young ladies to take pupils."

"I don't understand you, Mr. Codicil," said Rose, bewildered.

"Then I will no longer keep you in suspense. Your poor cousin, Philip, is dead, and you inherit your grandfather's fortune— that is, you, your sister, and brother."

"When did poor Philip die?" asked Rose, unaffectedly shocked. "It must have been very sudden."

"On the contrary, he died last year."

"Last year! How happens it, then, that we did not know of it before?"

"Because there has been a wicked scheme to defraud you of the inheritance. Ben, come here."

Ben entered, and the story was soon told. Of course it need not be repeated.

"Now, Miss Beaufort, if you insist on taking pupils, I will do what I can to procure you some," said the lawyer.

"If I take them it will be without compensation," answered Rose, smiling. "Can you tell me how soon we may expect to come into our property? I ask, because we are near the end of our money."

"It will take perhaps two months to obtain legal proof of Philip's death, but that will not inconvenience you. I will advance you whatever money you require in the meantime."

"You are very kind. If you could let me have twenty dollars——"

"You are very modest," said the lawyer, smiling. "Suppose we say two hundred?"

"Two hundred!" ejaculated Rose.

"I think you will be able to find a use for it," said the lawyer. "Remember, though I don't want to encourage you in extravagance, that is less than two weeks' income."

"There was great joy in the Beaufort household when Rose carried home the great news, though it was mingled with sorrow for the untimely fate of poor Philip.

CHAPTER XXXVII.

BEN MEETS HIS COUSIN.

BEN supposed that his new guardian would be in favor of making an immediate call upon his uncle, but the Cuban counselled delay.

"First," he said, "I wish to find, if I can, the broker through whom your uncle sold the securities of which he robbed your father. We can make out a case without it, but with this our case will be complete."

"Won't it be difficult to find out, Mr. Novarro?" asked Ben.

"Difficult, but not impossible. To begin with, I know the date of probable transfer. Next, I know the securities. By visiting the offices of different brokers I may obtain some information. At any rate, I have mapped out my plan of procedure, and hope within a week to obtain a clew."

20

Ben asked no questions, feeling that he could safely leave the whole matter in the hands of so experienced a business man as his new guardian.

They did not go to a hotel, but to a boarding-house kept by a Cuban lady, a friend of his guardian, which they found quite as comfortable and more homelike than the Metropolitan or the Windsor.

Meanwhile Ben thought it best not to make a call at the office of his uncle. Indeed, remembering the cruel way in which he had wronged his mother, he would have found it disagreeable to meet him.

But one day, on Broadway, he met his cousin, Clarence Plantagenet. He would have avoided the encounter, but it was too late, for Clarence had seen him.

"What! Ben!" he exclaimed. "I had no idea you were back in New York. When did you arrive?"

"Three days since," answered Ben.

"Where are you staying?"

"At a boarding-house in Forty-second street."

" How is Major Grafton ?"

"I don't know ; I am no longer with him."

" What !" exclaimed Clarence, pricking up his ears. " You are no longer in his employ ?"

" No."

" Where is he ?"

" I left him in Europe."

" What did he discharge you for ?" asked Clarence, cheerfully.

" He didn't discharge me. He was opposed to my leaving him, but we couldn't agree."

"I think you are a fool !" said Clarence, bluntly. " With him you could live like a gentleman. You haven't got another place, have you ?"

" No."

"And you won't get one very soon, I can tell you that, except as a boy at three or four dollars a week."

Ben smiled.

"I can look round, at any rate," he answered.

" That's all the good it'll do. You mustn't expect my father to help you."

"I don't.   If I had, I should have called before this."

"After throwing up a good place, if you were not discharged, you don't deserve help."

"I am not sure that I shall look for another place," said Ben.

"You are not?" asked Clarence, mystified.

"No; I may go to school a little longer.   I haven't as good an education as I should like."

"But how are you going to live while you are doing all this?"

"Don't you think your father would give me a home in his family and let me attend school in the city?"

"Well, Ben Baker, you have got cheek, I declare!   If that is what you are counting on, you may as well give it up."

"It's as well to know the worst," said Ben, tranquilly.

"I shall have to be going along," said Clarence, coldly.

He told his father at dinner about his meeting with Ben.

"I'll tell you what, father," he said.   "I couldn't account at first for Ben's seeming so cool and independent. I think I understand it now."

"Well, suppose you explain, then."

"I think he's robbed Major Grafton of a sum of money and taken French leave. He said he was not 'bounced,' and that the major did not want him to leave."

"I hope you are wrong, my son. I haven't the highest opinion of your cousin, but I earnestly hope he is honest. To have him guilty of such a crime would be a disgrace to our family. Always be honest, Clarence! Depend upon it, honesty is the best policy, and a boy or man makes a great mistake who appropriates what is not his own."

"Of course, pa, I know all that. Do you think I would steal? As to Ben Baker, that's a different matter. He's always been poor, and I suppose the temptation was too strong for him."

"Let us hope not. Dishonesty I could not overlook, even in a relation."

Who would imagine that this man, so strict in his ideas of honesty, had deliberately stolen a hundred thousand dollars from his widowed sister and her son!

CHAPTER XXXVIII.

MAJOR GRAFTON was quite easy in mind after consigning Ben to the safe custody of an insane asylum.

"Serves the boy right!" he said. "What business had he to interfere with my plans? M. Bourdon will see that he does not annoy me any further."

His confidence in the wisdom of his plan was maintained by the frequent letters he received from the director of the asylum, in all of which he spoke encouragingly of the effect of discipline upon Ben. Major Grafton regularly transmitted the compensation agreed on between them.

This continued until one day Major Grafton, who had now returned to Geneva, was dumfounded by receiving the following telegram from Mr. Codicil:

"Your scheme is revealed, and your guardianship at an end. No further drafts of yours will be honored. M. CODICIL."

"Confusion! What does this mean?" ejaculated Major Grafton. "That wretched boy must have found means of writing to America. If this is so, I will haul M. Bourdon over the coals. It must have been through his criminal negligence."

He lost no time in setting out for the asylum, which he reached in due season.

"I wish to see M. Bourdon," he said, sternly, to the attendant who had admitted him.

The doctor, who would rather have seen any one else, could hardly conceal his dismay when he set eyes on the major.

"Can he have found out?" he asked.

"Dr. Bourdon, how is my ward?" he demanded.

"Tranquil and contented," answered the doctor, smoothly.

"I have reason to think you have been negligent, and allowed him to write letters to America."

"Impossible, my dear sir—quite impossible,
I assure you."

"I believe there is some trickery here," said
the major, sternly.   "I wish to see the boy."

Perspiration gathered on the brow of M.
Bourdon, though it was a cool day. How
could he stave off this visit? His wits came
to the rescue.

"I greatly regret to tell you," he said, "that
your ward is sick of a contagious disease. To
see him would imperil your life."

Major Grafton was not a nervous man, and
he was too much in earnest to be turned from
his design.

"I am not afraid," he said; "I will see
him."

"I will go and prepare him for your visit,"
said the doctor, sorely perplexed.

Five minutes had not elapsed when he returned in apparent consternation.

"My good sir," he said, "I have serious
news. Your ward is not in his room. He
must have escaped in the night."

"You scoundrel!" exclaimed the major,
livid with passion. "Just now you told me

he was sick with a dangerous malady; now you say he has escaped. I have a great mind to strangle you!" and he clutched the doctor by the collar.

"Mercy, mercy!" shrieked the doctor, terribly alarmed. "Are you mad?"

"When did the boy escape? Tell me instantly, if you value your life."

"Over a month since. I didn't wish to alarm you, and so concealed the intelligence."

"While you continued to draw for his board, you thief!"

"I—I am prepared to refund the money, monsieur. I only drew because it was necessary to keep up the deception."

M. Bourdon refunded five weeks' board, told the story of Ben's escape, and Major Grafton was compelled to be content with this.

"I am afraid the game is up!" he muttered, as he rode rapidly away. "That cursed boy has spoiled all. I wish I had him in my clutches!"

It was well for Ben that he was not within reach of the irate major.

CHAPTER XXXIX.

BEN AND HIS UNCLE.

"BEN," said the Cuban, a few days later, "I have excellent news."

"What is it, sir?"

"I have found the broker who sold the stolen securities for your uncle."

"Is it possible, sir?" said Ben in excitement.

"Yes; it is a piece of great good luck. And now I think we are ready to call upon your uncle. First, however, I have a little scheme in which I shall require your co-operation."

"Very well, sir."

"I wish to test your uncle's disposition toward you. We are in a position to dictate terms to him. If he shows proper feeling toward his nephew we shall feel disposed to be considerate toward him."

"What do you wish me to do?" asked Ben.

"Call on your uncle and ask him if he can give you a place in his store, or help you to one outside. Of course you wouldn't accept one, but we shall see what reception he gives you."

Into this scheme Ben readily entered. He was no longer a friendless and penniless boy, dependent upon his uncle for the means of living, but rich and his own master.

Nicholas Walton was sitting in his counting-room when Ben entered. It so happened that Clarence Plantagenet was just leaving the store as Ben entered.

"What do you want?" he asked, coldly.

"I should like to see your father."

"I don't think he will see you. He is busy."

"I am quite anxious to see him," persisted Ben.

"Are you going to ask him to help you?" said his cousin.

"Yes; to help me to a place."

"I am sure he won't do it."

"I would rather take the refusal from his lips," said Ben.

"Oh, well, I suppose you can go and see him if you want to, but you will find that I am right."

"I think I will see him, then."

Clarence had been intending to go out at once, but it struck him that he would enjoy seeing his poor cousin rebuffed, and he accompanied Ben to the back of the store.

"Father," he said, as he entered the office, followed by Ben, "here is Ben Baker, who wants to see you. I told him it would be of no use to ask you for help, but he dosen't believe me."

Mr. Walton frowned ominously.

"Well, boy," he said, frigidly, "so you have lost your place with Major Grafton?"

"Yes, sir."

"I am convinced that it was on account of misconduct on your part."

"Is it quite right to condemn me before you have heard anything of the circumstances attending my leaving him?" said Ben, mildly.

"Oh, I dare say you have some plausible story," sneered Mr. Walton; "but it won't produce any effect on me."

"Still, sir, I will venture to say that I did not leave him on account of any misconduct on my own part."

"Perhaps it was on account of misconduct on his part," said Mr. Walton, with a scornful laugh.

"Yes, sir, it was."

"Really, this is very amusing. Now let me know what you want of me."

"Can you give me a place in your store, sir?"

"No, I can't, or rather I will not," answered his uncle, curtly.

"Will you use your influence to obtain me a position elsewhere?"

"No, I won't, and I consider you very impudent to prefer the request."

"You seem to forget, sir, that I am your nephew."

"I chose to forget it, considering the disreputable manner in which you have behaved."

"Then, you won't do anything for me, sir?"

"No, decidedly no!"

"I told you so," said Clarence, triumphantly. "You may as well go to selling papers."

"He can do better than that," said a strange voice. "He can live on the interest of his money."

Clarence and his father started in surprise, as the speaker, Filippo Novarro, entered the office. The merchant, recognizing him, turned pale.

CHAPTER XL.

CONCLUSION.

"I SEE you know me, Mr. Walton," said the Cuban, quietly. "I have a few words to say to you. Do you wish your son to listen ?"

"Clarence, you may leave the office," said the merchant, in a husky voice.

Clarence, whose curiosity was aroused, was very unwilling to go.

"Sha'n't Ben go, too?" he asked.

"Yes."

"I beg pardon, but I wish him to remain," said the Cuban. "He is deeply concerned in what I have to say."

Clarence was still more curious. He left the office, but he lingered within ear-shot.

"Mr. Walton," said Novarro, "I am a man of few words, and will come to the point. As the guardian of this boy, and the friend of his father's friend, I have come to demand from you the fortune of which you deprived him."

"I don't know what you are talking about," said the merchant, trying to speak firmly.

"I beg your pardon, but you do. I call for the money you obtained for the securities which you took from the dead body of Dr. Baker, who died in your house of heart disease—a sum which you appropriated to your own use, leaving your sister and your sister's son poor and dependent."

"You must be crazy, sir. Where is the proof of your strange and unfounded charge?"

"I can produce the broker who sold these securities for you in the year 18—."

"It is easy to say this. May I know the name of this broker?" asked the merchant, making a feeble attempt to deny the charge.

"His name is John Goldsmith, and his office is No. —— Wall street," answered Novarro, promptly.

Nicholas Walton leaned back in his chair and seemed ready to faint, but uttered no word.

"Well, sir, your answer?"

"Can't we — compromise — this — thing?" asked Walton, feebly.

"No, sir; we will promise not to expose you, but it will be only upon condition that you pay principal and interest. The only favor we will extend is, that we will not demand compound interest."

"But it will ruin me! I cannot take so large a sum from my business."

"That I can understand. In behalf of my young ward and his mother, I will agree to accept half cash, and half in notes maturing at different dates, secured by your stock in trade. Do you consent, or shall we bring suit?"

"Can't you throw off the interest? That boy and his mother will be amply provided for by the principal."

"If you had received your nephew differently when he applied for help just now, we might have consented. Now it is out of the question."

Nicholas Walton was forced to make an unconditional surrender, and the terms were agreed to upon the spot.

"Ben," said Mr. Novarro, as they left the office, "I congratulate you. You are now rich."

"Thanks to you kind management, Mr. Novarro."

It is said that listeners never hear any good of themselves. Clarence was in a terrible panic when he heard the conference between his father and the Cuban. That his despised cousin Ben should become suddenly rich was a bitter pill to swallow. He sneaked out of the store, perturbed in mind.

"Now, Ben, I suppose you will want to carry the news to your mother," said the Cuban.

"That is what I was about to ask, Mr. Novarro."

"We will take the next train for Sunderland, preparing your mother by a telegram."

I do not propose to describe Ben's happy meeting with his mother. Mrs. Baker was grieved to hear of her brother's treachery, but it was a relief to her to think that he had nothing to do with her husband's death. As we know, he was directly responsible for it, but the knowledge of this was confined to his own breast. Even the Cuban never suspected what had brought on the attack that terminated the poor doctor's life.

"Now, Ben, what career do you select?" asked his guardian.

Ben took a week to consider. He then decided not to go into business, but to obtain a liberal education, and study law. He and his mother removed to Cambridge, where he completed his preparatory studies, and entered Harvard College. He is now a young lawyer, and has commenced the practice of his profession under flattering auspices.

Clarence Plantagenet, on the other hand, is a young man about town, and his father cannot induce him to enter upon any business. He has professed his willingness to become a broker, if his father will purchase him a seat at the Stock Board, but Mr. Walton wisely thinks it will be cheaper to give him a liberal income than give him the chance of squandering a fortune in stocks.

We must not forget the Beauforts. They removed to a fashionable locality, and purchasing a house, furnished it with elegance and taste. It is surprising how many people found them out in their days of prosperity who had ignored them before. Even Mrs. Tilton essayed to apologize for her outrageous treatment, and tried to ingratiate herself with Rose, but the latter treated her with such distant civility that she gave up the attempt. In less than a year Rose Beaufort became Mrs. Clinton Randall, and her star rose still higher.

There is one person who never will forgive her for her good fortune, and that is Miss Arethusa Jayne, who had strongly hoped to secure the hand of Clinton Randall for herself. No one would have been more amazed than Randall himself, for he was happily unconscious of Miss Jayne's admiration for him.

Ben has not forgotten his early friends. Hugh Manton, the reporter, by his help has secured an interest in a flourishing daily paper in an inland city, and is earning a liberal income.

Major Grafton is earning a precarious living

at European spas and gambling resorts, and is beginning to show the marks of age. Filippo Novarro has established himself as a permanent resident of the United States, and spends much of his time with Ben and his mother.

And now, with all our characters satisfactorily disposed of, the good rewarded, and the bad punished, we bid the reader farewell and ring down the curtain.

HORATIO ALGER, JR.

The enormous sales of the books of Horatio Alger, Jr., show the greatness of his popularity among the boys, and prove that he is one of their most favored writers. I am told that more than half a million copies altogether have been sold, and that all the large circulating libraries in the country have several complete sets, of which only two or three volumes are ever on the shelves at one time. If this is true, what thousands and thousands of boys have read and are reading Mr. Alger's books! His peculiar style of stories, often imitated but never equaled, have taken a hold upon the young people, and, despite their similarity, are eagerly read as soon as they appear.

Mr. Alger became famous with the publication of that undying book, "Ragged Dick, or Street Life in New York." It was his first book for young people, and its success was so great that he immediately devoted himself to that kind of writing. It was a new and fertile field for a writer then, and Mr. Alger's treatment of it at once caught the fancy of the boys. "Ragged Dick" first appeared in 1868, and ever since then it has been selling steadily, until now it is estimated that about 200,000 copies of the series have been sold.

—"Pleasant Hours for Boys and Girls."

A writer for boys should have an abundant sympathy with them. He should be able to enter into their plans, hopes, and aspirations. He should learn to look upon life as they do. Boys object to be written down to. A boy's heart opens to the man or writer who understands him.

—From "Writing Stories for Boys," by Horatio Alger, Jr.

RAGGED DICK SERIES.

6 vols.   By Horatio Alger, Jr. $6.00

Ragged Dick.	Rough and Ready.
Fame and Fortune.	Ben the Luggage Boy.
Mark the Match Boy.	Rufus and Rose.

TATTERED TOM SERIES—First Series.

4 vols.   By Horatio Alger, Jr. $4.00

Tattered Tom.	Phil the Fiddler.
Paul the Peddler.	Slow and Sure.

TATTERED TOM SERIES—Second Series.

4 vols. $4.00

Julius.	Sam's Chance.
The Young Outlaw.	The Telegraph Boy.

CAMPAIGN SERIES.

3 vols.   By Horatio Alger, Jr. $3.00

Frank's Campaign.	Charlie Codman's Cruise.
Paul Prescott's Charge.	

LUCK AND PLUCK SERIES—First Series.

4 vols.   By Horatio Alger, Jr. $4.00

Luck and Pluck.	Strong and Steady.
Sink or Swim.	Strive and Succeed.

LUCK AND PLUCK SERIES—Second Series.

4 vols. $4.00

Try and Trust.	Risen from the Ranks.
Bound to Rise.	Herbert Carter's Legacy.

BRAVE AND BOLD SERIES.

4 vols.   By Horatio Alger, Jr. $4.00

Brave and Bold.	Shifting for Himself.
Jack's Ward.	Wait and Hope.

COMPLETE CATALOG OF BEST BOOKS FOR BOYS AND GIRLS
MAILED ON APPLICATION TO THE PUBLISHERS
THE JOHN C. WINSTON CO., PHILADELPHIA

VICTORY SERIES.

3 vols.   By Horatio Alger, Jr. $3.00

Only an Irish Boy.   Adrift in the City.

Victor Vane, or the Young Secretary.

FRANK AND FEARLESS SERIES.

3 vols.   By Horatio Alger, Jr. $3.00

Frank Hunter's Peril.   Frank and Fearless.

The Young Salesman.

GOOD FORTUNE LIBRARY.

3 vols.   By Horatio Alger, Jr. $3.00

Walter Sherwood's Probation. A Boy's Fortune.

The Young Bank Messenger.

HOW TO RISE LIBRARY.

3 vols.   By Horatio Alger, Jr. $3.00

Jed, the Poorhouse Boy.   Rupert's Ambition.

Lester's Luck.

COMPLETE CATALOG OF BEST BOOKS FOR BOYS AND GIRLS
MAILED ON APPLICATION TO THE PUBLISHERS

THE JOHN C. WINSTON CO., PHILADELPHIA

FAMOUS STANDARD JUVENILES
FOR GIRLS
A GOOD GIRL'S BOOK IS HARD TO FIND!

One often hears the above quoted. *These* books have stood the tests of time and careful mothers, and will be of the greatest interest to girls of all ages. Free from any unhealthy sensationalism, yet full of incident and romance, they are the cream of the best girls' books published. These volumes, each one well illustrated, carefully printed on excellent paper, substantially bound in cloth, 12mo.

WAYS AND MEANS LIBRARY. By Margaret Vandegrift. 4 vols. $3 00
Queen's Body Guard.   Doris and Theodora.
Rose Raymond's Wards.   Ways and Means.

STORIES FOR GIRLS. 3 vols. 2 25
Dr. Gilbert's Daughters.
Marion Berkley.   Hartwell Farm.

HONEST ENDEAVOR LIBRARY. By Lucy C. Lillie. 3 vols. $2 25
The Family Dilemma.   Allison's Adventures.
Ruth Endicott's Way.

MILBROOK LIBRARY. By Lucy C. Lillie.
4 vols. $3 00
Helen Glenn.   Esther's Fortune.
The Squire's Daughter. For Honor's Sake.

RECENT SUCCESSES

The following, though of recent date, have at once reached such a height of popularity that they can already be classified as standards. 75 cents each.

Lady Green Satin.   By Baroness Deschesney.
Marion Berkley. By Elizabeth B. Comins.
Lenny, the Orphan.   By Margaret Hosmer.
Family Dilemma. By Lucy C. Lillie.
Question of Honor. By Lynde Palmer
Girl's Ordeal, A. By Lucy C. Lillie.
Elinor Belden; or The Step Brothers. By Lucy C. Lillie.
Where Honor Leads. By Lynde Palmer.
Under the Holly. By Margaret Hosmer.
Two Bequests. The; or, Heavenward Led. By Jane R. Sommers.
The Thistles of Mount Cedar. By Ursula Tannenforst. · - $1.25

Catalogue sent on application to the Publisher

A Veritable "Arabian Nights" of Entertainment
Containing 168 Complete Illustrated Stories.

HURLBUT'S STORY OF THE BIBLE

told for

YOUNG AND OLD

by

Rev. Jesse Lyman Hurlbut, D.D.

THE BIBLE MADE FASCINATING TO CHILDREN.—The heroes and the noble men and women of the Bible are made to appear as living, acting people. The book is an original work, and in no sense an imitation. It has been in preparation for a number of years.

THE DISTINGUISHED AUTHOR.—Dr. Hurlbut has long been associated with, and director of, the Sunday School work of one of the largest denominations, and he has been more closely associated with the detail work of the Chautauqua movement than has any other man. He is also well known as a writer.

REMARKABLE FOR THE BEAUTY AND NUMBER OF ITS ILLUSTRATIONS.—There are sixteen pictures in color prepared for this work by the distinguished artist, W. H. Margetson, and reproduced with the beauty and attractiveness of the artist's original work. There are also **nearly 300 half-tone** engravings in this remarkable book, which is as original in the selection of its illustrations as it is in its stories.

WHAT OTHERS THINK OF IT

"It is a needed and original work. Not an imitation."—*Christian Advocate*, New York.

"Written in such a style as to fascinate and hold the interest of child or man."—REV. F. E. CLARK, Pres. Society of Christian Endeavor.

"It is a beautiful book. I hope every family in the land will secure 'Hurlbut's Story of the Bible.' "—GENERAL O. O. HOWARD.

"The best book of its kind, and that kind the most important."—REV. JAMES A. WORDEN, Presbyterian B'd of Pub. and S. S. Work.

"I like very much the vocabulary you have used, and I can see how careful you have been in choosing understandable words."—MR. PHILIP E. HOWARD, *Sunday-School Times*, Philadelphia.

"It is the completest and best thing of the kind I have seen. The book is splendidly illustrated." MARIAN LAWRANCE, General Secretary International Sunday-School Association.

"Many will be drawn to the Bible who otherwise might look upon it as only adapted for older people."—HON. DAVID J. BREWER, Justice of the Supreme Court of the United States.

8vo, cloth. 750 pages. 16 color plates. 262 half-tone engravings. **Net $1.50**

The JOHN C. WINSTON CO.

THE RENOWNED STANDARD JUVENILES
BY EDWARD S. ELLIS

Edward S. Ellis is regarded as the later day Cooper. His books will always be read for the accurate pen pictures of pioneer life they portray.

LIST OF TITLES

DEERFOOT SERIES
Hunters of the Ozark.
The Last War Trail.
Camp in the Mountains.

LOG CABIN SERIES
Lost Trail.
Footprints in the Forest.
Camp Fire and Wigwam.

BOY PIONEER SERIES
Ned in the Block-House.
Ned on the River.
Ned in the Woods.

THE NORTHWEST SERIES
Two Boys in Wyoming.
Cowmen and Rustlers.
A Strange Craft and Its Wonderful Voyage.

BOONE AND KENTON SERIES
Shod with Silence.
In the Days of the Pioneers.
Phantom of the River.

WAR CHIEF SERIES
Red Eagle.
Blazing Arrow.
Iron Heart, War Chief of the Iroquois.

THE NEW DEERFOOT SERIES
Deerfoot in the Forest.
Deerfoot on the Prairie.
Deerfoot in the Mountains.

TRUE GRIT SERIES
Jim and Joe.
Dorsey, the Young Inventor.
Secret of Coffin Island.

GREAT AMERICAN SERIES
Teddy and Towser; or, Early Days in California.
Up the Forked River.

COLONIAL SERIES
An American King.
The Cromwell of Virginia.
The Last Emperor of the Old Dominion.

FOREIGN ADVENTURE SERIES
Lost in the Forbidden Land.
River and Jungle.
The Hunt of the White Elephant.

PADDLE YOUR OWN CANOE SERIES
The Forest Messengers.
The Mountain Star.
Queen of the Clouds.

ARIZONA SERIES
Off the Reservation; or, Caught in an Apache Raid.
Trailing Geronimo; or, Campaigning with Crook.
The Round-Up; or, Geronimo's Last Raid.

OTHER TITLES IN PREPARATION

PRICE $1.00 PER VOLUME   Sold separately and in set

Complete Catalogue of Famous Alger Books, Celebrated Castlemon Books and Renowned Ellis Books mailed on application.

THE JOHN C. WINSTON CO.   PHILADELPHIA, PA.

www.ingramcontent.com/pod-product-compliance
Lightning Source LLC
Chambersburg PA
CBHW020933030726
47496CB00005B/1169